DEPRAVITY

M.J. HAAG

ISBN 978-0-988852-37-2 (eBook Edition)
ISBN 978-1-943051-19-9 (Paperback Edition)
ISBN 978-1-514288-55-9 (CreateSpace Paperback Edition)

Editing by Ulva Eldridge
Cover design by Shattered Glass Publishing LLC

To all the hours I spent reading historical novels as a teen, thanks for the realism. Here's some magic.

CHAPTER ONE

I WRAPPED MY HANDS AROUND THE COLD BARS OF THE massive, black iron gate and glared after the smith's sons, Tennen and Splane Coalre. The pair cast nervous glances back at me as they scurried away from the beast's shadowy garden. They had locked me inside because of misdirected spite. It wasn't my fault I'd seen what I had.

"This is what you get, Benella," Tennen had said as he had pushed me into the beast's lair.

Tennen thought his treatment just. However, the current situation was anything but just.

A strand of my dark hair, loosened from my braid by the encounter, fell across my cheek and partially obstructed my view of my retreating tormentors. I shook the hair away from my eyes and took stock of my situation.

Outside the gate, early morning mist floated around the trunks of the trees, and blue sky shimmered through

M.J. HAAG

the gently moving canopy. Inside the gate, neither the light mist nor blue sky penetrated the garden in which I stood. Cast in shadow and eerie silence, the beast's domain welcomed nothing from beyond its walls.

Sides still heaving, I struggled to quiet my breathing. I needed to leave quickly. Tennen and Splane hadn't departed quietly, and it wouldn't be long before the creature came looking for me.

I studied the top of the gate. The iron should have been easy enough to scale, but vines climbed the rock walls and twined with the iron rods. I didn't trust the vines. They tended to move on their own. I didn't much trust the gate, either. It should have been closed and locked.

The birds outside the gate fell eerily silent, and my stomach gave a sickening twist as I realized I'd run out of time. I dropped my head and squeezed my eyes shut.

The beast had come.

A heavy breath gusted across my neck, sending shivers of fear over my skin, and my hands twitched on the gate. In the distance, I heard the mocking laughter of the smith's sons as they raced home.

Taking a slow breath, I forced my fingers from the bars and dropped my hands to my sides. I didn't turn to look at the beast. I didn't need to. Once before, I'd seen his dark shape hidden in mist when strangers, worked into a righteous fit, had come to Konrall and tried to storm the estate.

My breath left me when he clasped my arms, and I suddenly found myself sailing over the wall. I flipped, spun, then floated for a moment before I felt myself drawn back to earth.

I braced myself for the bone-jarring collision. Instead, I bounced slightly on impact. Puzzled, I quickly sat up. A woven mesh of vines strung between trees had cushioned me from the hard landing I had expected. I scrambled off and turned to stare at the tangled vegetation that had saved me. The vines slithered back from the trees, releasing their hold on each other. Slowly, they withdrew to disappear over the wall from where they'd come.

I stood panting and shaking, looking at the stone wall that extended beyond sight in each direction. The bars I'd held only a moment ago broke the monotony of the stonescape far to my left. He'd tossed me a good distance. Had it not been for the vines, I would have broken a limb or worse.

My stomach growled hungrily as I bent to inspect my clothes. Father couldn't afford to replace them. Other than dirt and a few small tears, which I could mend, the old worn pants and shirt would last a while longer. I sighed and straightened.

The day hadn't started well. I'd set out to trade for bread using the wild carrots I'd foraged at dawn. Carrots, typically a fall crop, were easy to find in early spring if one knew where to look. The beast's enchanted gardens grew year round. Though he allowed no one inside, a clever girl could still benefit from the estate. On the east side of the property, the plants crept through a section of crumbling wall. Amidst the fallen rocks, I could find any variety of fruit or vegetable. The type changed every day, depending on the mood of the magic.

After the long walk back to town with the crisp roots in my bag, I had waited by the baker's side door, hidden behind one of the discarded barrels littering his yard. Through the gaps in the roughly boarded walls, the heat from the ovens warmed my face as I watched the baker move around his kitchen.

Sweat had already dampened his brown hair and the heat had colored his face. The white apron that covered his girth was well dusted with flour as he worked at the large wooden table, rolling dough and adding ingredients. The smell of yeast and baking bread filled my cramped hiding spot outside.

He lifted something to his mouth and chewed. His jowls jiggled with his jerky bites as he squinted thoughtfully. He sampled everything. When I was younger, I'd asked him why. He'd winked, in a secretive way that made me feel uncomfortable, and said he needed to sample in order to know if the goods were quality.

I didn't care for the baker. That's why I hid in the alley, hoping for a glimpse of his mother. She was kind enough to trade carrots for bread while the baker didn't care how hungry a person was unless they had coin. My father, sisters, and I often went without bread because of it.

As I crouched, waiting for the baker's mother, the smith's wife, Sara, timidly knocked at the baker's door. I saw him smile before moving to answer the door.

"Come in, dear lady," he said, backing up to let Sara enter.

I found it odd that she used the side door. The shop, filled with the goods for sale, ran along the front of the building and had its own entry.

"How's business at the smithy?" he asked in a cordial tone.

"You know it's no better or Patrick wouldn't have sent me," Sara said.

I wondered why Sara's husband had sent her to the baker if their business was slow.

"That's too bad," he said, clearing his dough from the table. "The price has gone up."

"What?" Sara said in a shocked gasp.

"Don't fret. You'll be able to pay, I'm sure. I've looked my fill, you see."

With the table cleared, he moved to Sara and helped her remove her jacket. Though an older woman, she still held her beauty. I'd heard many men in town comment on her pretty features and gentle bearing.

"A taste. That's all I ask. If you don't want to mention

the increase to Patrick, I'll not mention it, either, though I don't think he'd mind."

Sara chewed on her lip and struggled with threatening tears. She watched the baker as he laid a cloth on the flour-dusted table. Then he gave a single, curt nod, backed her up to the table, and helped her sit upon it.

I wondered what they were about. My curiosity held me in place as I continued to peer through a small crack in the wall, so that I might find out.

"As I promised Patrick in the beginning, I'll not lay a hand on you." The baker walked to the door that separated the bakery from the shop and locked it. Then he locked the side door.

"Flip back your skirts."

Sara lay back on the table and did as she was told. I was shocked to see bare legs and no underthings, but I began to understand the baker's price. At sixteen, though still innocent, I was far from naive. I'd spied my sister, Bryn, kissing Tennen on occasion. A loose blouse and a hand on her breast usually accompanied the kiss.

"Draw your heels up to the table, and drop your knees to the side so I can see you better," the baker said in a husky voice. I could see a bulge under his apron as he watched Sara do what she'd been told.

He dropped to his knees, kneeling between her splayed legs. My view became slightly obstructed by her foot, but I saw and heard enough to know he licked her. Repeatedly.

Sara started making little gasping noises, and I wondered if it hurt.

True to his word, the baker didn't lay a hand on her, but he did on himself. He reached under his apron and began tugging on himself. His grunts mingled with her gasps. The sounds they made remained muffled until the end when they both increased in volume for just a moment. Then, silence fell. The baker gave Sara one final slurp and rose to wash his hands.

My cheeks flamed from what I'd just witnessed, and I felt sick.

Sara sat up, equally flushed. She refused to look at the baker as she straightened her skirts and stood on shaky legs. The baker wrapped a large loaf of bread, fresh out of the oven, and handed it to her.

I didn't want to stay and hear anymore. Silently, I rose and crept from my hiding spot, willing to wait for another day to catch the baker's mother. My list of reasons to avoid the baker had just grown.

That was when I turned the corner and ran into Tennen and Splane. They had both been leaning against the neighboring building, waiting for their mother. Neither had noticed me at first, until Tennen ran his hand through his dark hair. Splane's golden head was turned to study his brother, until Tennen froze.

The pair had taken one look at my face, somehow sensed I had seen their mother with the baker, and had started toward me. Forgetting about the carrots in the pouch slung across my shoulders, I'd run, and they'd given chase.

A chase that could have ended much worse, I thought.

Sighing, I checked that the carrots were undamaged from my fall, grabbed one out, and started munching on it as I walked. There'd be no going back to the baker's today. I hoped Bryn would be able to make something of the carrots.

Birds chattered around me, and the mist dissipated the closer I came to home. The trees thinned, and I spotted the curling wisps of smoke from Konrall's chimneys ahead. At our cottage on the outskirts of the village, I wiped my feet on the rug before letting myself inside.

The smell of breakfast surrounded me and, despite the carrot I had eaten, my stomach growled again. Bryn stood before the stove, stirring something. Everything else was quiet. I glanced around. Two cups sat near the edge of the sink. Father and Blye had already left for work.

"Any luck this morning?" Bryn asked as she plated an egg and some greens for me.

"No bread. But I do have a lovely bunch of carrots." I set the carrots on the table and sat at one of the four chairs.

I lived at home with my father, Benard, and my two sisters, Bryn and Blye. Father taught the local children for a modest fee, and Blye helped the seamstress. What little money Blye brought home, she gave to Father. Mostly,

Blye received scraps of lace and ribbon as payment, which she kept in a box in our room. She was clever with a needle and thread. So much so, that no one could tell I wore hand off clothes from my sisters.

"Mr. Medunge wasn't cooperating again?" Bryn asked.

She knew the baker didn't often trade. He required coin. Except this morning. I stirred the eggs on my plate, wondering if I should mention what I'd witnessed. I wasn't even sure if I could talk about it, but shouldn't someone know that Mr. Medunge had gone too far? I recalled Sara's face, flushed and uncomfortable with a trace of disgust when she had stood. She wouldn't like anyone knowing what she'd done for bread, so I kept the tale to myself.

"I didn't bother with him. It's easier if I wait for Mrs. Medunge."

Bryn cleaned up breakfast from the stove then turned toward me.

"If you have no plans for today, would you circle the estate? We're running low on just about everything."

I glanced at the shelves near the stove. Crocks and cloth sacks lined the aged wood planks. Granted, a few of the sacks drooped loosely at the tops, but they weren't empty. It took a moment for me to realize it wasn't supplies she wanted but my absence.

Bryn had it in her head that Tennen, the same Tennen who'd locked me in the beast's garden, would make her a fine husband. She thought the Coalre family was wealthy and wanted a comfortable life. Little did she know. However, I needed no further motivation to eat quickly and bring my plate to the sink. I didn't want another run-in with Tennen or Splane so soon.

Because of Bryn's unshakeable infatuation with Tennen, I didn't bother telling her what he'd done. Any remotely negative remark toward the Coalre family would result in retribution from Bryn, usually in the form of inedible food.

Taking the fresh carrots from the bag, I searched the sacks on the shelf for any aging vegetables. Wilted greens caught my eye, and I swapped them for the carrots. Calling out a farewell to my sister, I left her to her affairs and once again trekked toward the beast's estate.

I didn't mind the time I spent outdoors. It was a vastly acceptable pastime compared to my sisters' chosen occupations. Sewing for an extended period numbed my mind, as did cleaning and cooking. Amongst the trees, however, opportunity for adventure abounded.

In the woods, just before entering the thicker mists, I set several snares with the wilted greens. I'd learned long ago not to set my traps any closer to the estate. Odd things happened to them if I did. I often found the ropes chewed to pieces and, once, animal feces in place of the bait in the exact center of the unsprung trap. It didn't take long for me to determine the vegetation wasn't the only thing enchanted around the estate.

With the snares set and nothing else to do, I went to the nearby stream that ran perpendicular to the estate, flowing south near Konrall. Since most people didn't venture this close to the estate, I enjoyed enough privacy for a swim. Clothed, of course, since the waters still ran cold; and I didn't trust Splane to stay home while Bryn entertained Tennen. I didn't linger long.

Chilled and wet from my time in the water, I shivered as I walked my way around the estate, heading east. It typically took me most of the day to complete the circuit, but I didn't mind. Gradually, the wall curved north, and I passed the place where things usually grew. I was not surprised to see barren ground, even though I had picked only a third of what the estate had offered that morning. A third seemed more than a fair share to me, and the estate seemed to agree for, if I returned later in the day, as I did now, it never offered more.

At the northernmost point of the walled property, I spotted a unique flower growing from the mortar. Its roots barely clung to the hardened surface, but I didn't puzzle over it. I knew that anything was possible at the estate or near its wall. I plucked the flower, placed it in my bag, and continued on my way.

Several hours later, I came back to my traps and found I was lucky to have caught a fat rabbit. Its dull eyes let me know it'd been waiting for me awhile.

With the rabbit slung over my shoulder, I started home.

Bryn could make a wonderful rabbit stew, and I knew to look forward to it for breakfast.

At home, Bryn had already cleaned up dinner but had left a plate for me near the stove to keep it warm. She thanked me when I showed her the rabbit, but insisted I clean it before I ate. She didn't want it staring at her any longer than necessary.

Tired, hungry, and wanting to change out of my stiff clothes, I went to the back and cleaned the rabbit, keeping the skin for the butcher. The butcher, a kind man, took many different things in trade for meat. My luck with snares didn't often require me to visit the butcher, but it didn't stop me from helping him when I could. I had no use for the skins, but he cured them and sold them to traveling merchants or anyone else looking for leather or fur. It didn't amount to much money for him, but it did make it possible for him to be charitable to my family when the need arose.

With the carcass clean and the skin set to dry, I brought Bryn what she needed for the stew and sat down for my own rushed dinner. I hadn't forgotten the flower and wanted to ask my father about it.

My father, a brilliant man, often fell under the thrall of the books that lined his study walls and didn't hear me when I first knocked. I knocked a second time to get his attention. He looked up with a smile and motioned me in, setting his book to the side.

"What do you have there, Bini?" he asked.

I grinned at him, liking that he had used his pet name for me. It meant I had his full attention.

"I found this near the wall. Do you know what it is?" I handed the delicate flower to him.

"It's a primrose, dear. We don't see them here." He set the flower on his desk and stood, eyeing his shelves. "Let's see..." He moved to a section and took a book from its place. Flipping it open, he read for several moments, occasionally turning several pages at a time. "Here," he said, handing me the book.

In it, an artist had sketched a likeness of my flower. Once common to many places around the world, its numbers had dwindled as ladies, enraptured by its sweet smell, tore it from the ground in vast quantities to make perfume. I frowned at the book then at the flower. I shouldn't have picked it.

"I would think your sister, Bryn, would like the flower if you have no use for it. She could make a light scent from it. Very small, of course. Fun for her to try, no doubt," he said as he went back to his book.

I scooped up the wilted flower, replaced the book, and did as he suggested, feeling guilty.

WITH RELIEF, I tucked the warm loaf of bread into the

bag hanging from my shoulder. The crust crackled as I handled it, sending the yeasty smell into the air to tickle my nose; and I couldn't wait to get back to the cottage to show Bryn.

After two days of patiently waiting, I'd finally had a bit of luck. In need of a visit to the outhouse, the baker had called for his mother and asked her to watch the browning bread.

Mrs. Medunge called another thanks for the carrots and wild onions and waved a farewell from the side door. I spared her a brief wave in return and hurried from the cramped alley between the bakery and the baker's storage shed.

Konrall consisted of one main dirt road that divided the village north to south. To the north, it led to the next village, Water-On-The-Bridge, some twelve miles away. To the south, it led to farmlands and little else. But here, in the middle of the village, its stone filled ruts lent a clean look, as did the trim grass growing between the line of buildings on each side of the road.

It was a pleasant enough way to walk if it wouldn't have brought me too uncomfortably close to the blacksmith. I'd successfully avoided Tennen and Splane since our last run-in.

As I neared the butcher, Sara, flanked by Tennen and Splane, left the smithy and headed in my direction.

Panicking, I stepped through the butcher's open door, startling him.

"Ho, there, Bini!" cried Mr. Flune with a laugh. "Are you so hungry to come running through my door?"

"I'm sorry for startling you, Mr. Flune," I said. "I wanted to see if you found the hide I left at your door yesterday."

"I did indeed," he said with a kind smile. "It's a beauty. We don't see white fur often, so it will fetch a fine price." He stepped back from his butcher's block, away from the meat laid out for slicing, and reached for a small wrapped package. "This is for you, a trifling token of thanks for such a prize."

Smiling widely, I took the package, liking the mystery of it. He often gave me small things to take home, and I never knew what they might be. I thanked him and, after checking the road, went on my merry way, happy with the day's trades.

When I walked through the cottage door, Bryn was consoling a sobbing Blye.

"What's happened?" I asked. Blye should have been at work; the day had just started.

"The seamstress can't afford to pay me this month. There are too few orders."

Though Blye didn't earn much, what she did earn, helped. With that disheartening news, I pulled the bread from my bag and set it on the table.

"It's still warm," I said quietly to Bryn. I handed her the package, too, having already peeked at its contents. A dollop of pig fat glistened within.

Meanwhile, Blye continued to sniffle and sob. Though I considered the loss of her coin sad news, I didn't understand why Blye would choose to wail in self-pity rather than look for a solution. It was a waste of time to carry on as she was. At the very least, she should have faith our father would not let us fall into destitution.

"Blye, we'll pull through," I said. "We always do. Please stop crying. You don't want Father to come home and see you like this." Her gaze flashed with displeasure, but she wiped at her eyes. I took that as a good sign and continued trying to cheer her.

"You are clever with a needle and thread. And, you still have bits of the materials she's given you. You'll find something clever to do with those. I know you will. I'll probably see someone wearing a bit of it in their hair or on their breast next week."

Her eyes widened, and for a moment, I thought I'd offended her. But, she popped from her chair, a slow smile creeping onto her tear-stained face.

"You are the brilliant one, Benella. Their hair," she said excitedly. "I can make pieces to exactly match the existing dresses."

I had no idea what she meant but nodded my agreement. She dashed back to our room, saying she needed to start right away and that I should bring her anything pretty I found on my wanderings, like feathers and such.

"You always seem to find the right side and turn it up." Bryn shook her head then cut me a slice of the bread and spread a thin layer of our fresh butter on it. "Here. Take this with you. I know you'll want to walk around and find something for Blye right away."

I reached for the bread as she expected, even though I didn't really want to walk the estate so soon. Blye would appreciate anything I found, especially if I found it quickly. If I stayed, she would probably start crying again. Taking a bite of the bread, I grabbed my bag and left.

The dark woods surrounded me with a sense of peace. Many of the village folk didn't like foraging so close to the estate, and that made my foraging much quieter and easier. Before I reached the shadowy mists, I heard the cry of a large bird above me. I followed it with my eyes and watched it land on a forked branch of the largest tree in the area. Not far from its perch, I spotted a twig nest that was wedged in the crotch of the two branches. The bird ruffled its white and grey feathers and hopped forward to begin feeding its squawking young.

Wrinkling my nose, I eyed the bird's feathers then adjusted my bag and set to climbing the enormous tree. The bark bit into my hands and scraped the skin of my legs through my woolen trousers as I scrambled from branch to branch. The bird noticed my ascent and shrieked at me before taking flight.

Minutes later, I pulled myself onto the branch that held the nest and glanced at the tangle of twigs. Slowly, I inched forward, clinging to the branch so the wind didn't catch me unaware. The large chicks, blind to what approached them, chirped at me hopefully and opened their mouths wide. Soft down feathers the size of my hand lined the nest and cushioned the chicks. Those beautiful white feathers would be a prize in any lady's hair.

I removed several from the nest, careful not to touch anything else. I didn't want to scare the mother off or rob the babies of their warmth.

The climb down took much longer than the climb up, and my legs began to shake with the strain before I reached the ground. In the distance, I heard voices and worried they might be Tennen and Splane's. Despite the tiredness I felt, I hurriedly dropped the last few feet, managed to land softly, and quickly disappeared into the mists.

I traversed around the wall, finding more treasures. The place where the primrose had grown now had several more delicate flowers. Carefully, I plucked the buds, leaving the roots to grow. Bryn hadn't been able to make anything with the single flower, and I doubted she'd be able to do much with the six I'd just found, but the candle maker might.

Not far from the primrose, I discovered a large spider

spinning a silvery web. It noted my attention and spat web at me. I jumped back in surprise, and the web missed me and landed on the grass. It shimmered in the mist. Keeping an eye on the spider, I bent to touch the web. It didn't stick to my fingers. Instead, its strong silk slithered over them softly. It would make a fine thread. The spider didn't seem to notice me pulling the mass of web from the grass.

Hungry and tired, I returned home well after dinner. A covered plate waited for me in the quiet kitchen. Sitting to eat, I heard Bryn and Blye talking softly in our room and knew our father read in his study, as he did every night after dinner.

It didn't take my sisters long to come from the room and inquire after what I'd found. I set my food aside and pulled the thread and feathers from the bag. Blye exclaimed over the thread, asking where I'd found it. When I explained about the spider, she begged me to return the next day to try to get more. I nodded my agreement, and she left with her prizes to go sew.

THE CANDLE MAKER eagerly accepted the flowers, saying a scented candle was worth its weight in silver. Then, he sadly admitted he had nothing to give me in payment until it sold. Though disappointed, the lack of payment didn't stop me from looking for more flowers as I walked around the wall to find the spider. But the day didn't gift me with either of them. The primrose plants that I'd plucked free of any flowers the day before were completely gone. The spider, too, had vanished along with his pretty web. Even the patch that usually yielded some type of food had nothing. I eyed the wall sadly, wondering why it was being so uncooperative.

As I neared the gate to complete my journey around the estate, it swung open of its own accord. Heart thumping wildly in my chest, I froze and stared at the black iron, listening for the telltale sounds of the beast's approach. Nothing sounded but the wind. It puzzled me why the gate would open as it had. I didn't think it was an invitation. Especially when the wall hadn't been very bountiful like it usually was. Guilt struck at how much I'd taken over the last few days without giving anything in return. Usually, I only took carrots, onions, and the like. What if the estate expected compensation for the other things I'd taken? Worried that might be the case, I checked my bag for an offering but found nothing. With unease, I walked away.

The day grew pleasantly warm as I made my way home. When I neared, I went around back to check my own garden's progress. The onions were just sprouting little green tops, and the peas were an inch high. I hoped the warm weather would hold.

"Well, how much did you get?" Bryn's voice carried

through an open window.

I looked up in surprise. The voice had come from our shared bedroom window.

"A silver!" Blye said. I smiled, knowing they were talking about Blye's first hairpiece.

"And I'm hiding it in the usual spot," Blye continued. "I wish Benella didn't even know I'd been working on it. What if she mentions something to Father?"

My smile faded as I listened.

"We'll keep her busy searching for more things to use. It should be fine," Bryn said.

"I'll give the coin of every third sale to Father just like I did when that fat cow paid me. I still can't believe she said she couldn't afford to keep me on. I sew better than she does. She'll lose business fast now, I swear. I hate this town and refuse to be stuck here for the rest of my life."

"At least you can save decent coin to leave. What I've put aside in change from Father's food allowance is nothing in comparison," Bryn complained.

How could they withhold any coin from Father? He provided us with food and shelter and love. I didn't understand them.

"I told you, if you marry Tennen, you won't have to worry anyway. Their mother is one of Mrs. Stinich's best customers. They obviously have money."

Although the news that they were hiding coin away annoyed me, I refused to act on my emotions as impetuously as they did. Turning away from the window, I quietly walked around the house and entered through the front, making plenty of noise. Both came out with smiles and asked what I'd found. I didn't feel too badly when I admitted there was nothing.

"What about the web? Surely you could have taken that if the spider was gone," said Blye with a hint of reprimand.

"The spider took the web with him. There was nothing left."

She glowered at me for a moment before smoothing her face into a sympathetic expression. "Thank you for trying. The estate is fickle. Perhaps tomorrow will be better."

"Could you take some of the carrots to the bakery and see if you can trade for bread again?" Bryn asked, changing the subject.

"I'd rather not. It's hard to catch Mrs. Medunge, and the baker refuses to trade."

"I heard from Tennen that the baker looks kindly on you. I think you just need to ask again," Bryn said.

I really didn't want to approach the baker again.

"Is there nothing left of the coin we set aside for food?" I asked without a hint of recrimination.

"No," Bryn said, turning away. "I'll make do with a soup tonight, but meat and bread would be appreciated tomorrow."

CHAPTER TWO

I FORCED MYSELF TO APPROACH THE BAKER AFTER three days of little game or harvest from the estate. Taking my time, I walked to town with my bag slung across my chest. The wilting carrots thumped against my hip with each stone-kicking stride. Because of my musings and lack of concentration, I didn't see Tennen and Splane idling against the tinker's building until they spoke to me as I passed.

"Well, hello, Benella," Tennen said.

Startled, I turned to face him instead of ignoring him. His eyes narrowed on me. I looked around at the light foot traffic and saw no one near enough to help me. The baker's side door opened and Sara, looking flushed, stepped out with a loaf of bread.

My eyes darted from her to Tennen. He shook his head slowly.

"Bad timing," he said harshly.

My first instinct was to run, but I knew they would catch me before we cleared town. While trying to think of a way to avoid a beating, I gained the baker's attention, and he called to us.

"You boys walk your mother home. Benella, come inside and let's see what goods you have to sell."

Run and risk a beating or face the baker?

"Not so much better than the rest of us, now, are you?" Splane said softly.

His statement confused me. How had I ever given them the impression I thought of myself as better? I had crouched, hiding behind the crates by the baker's shop for hours, cold and hungry, waiting for Mrs. Medunge to appear. The whole village was poor with the exception of the baker. Shaking my head, I turned and walked toward the horrid man.

Sara didn't meet my eyes as I passed her, not that I blamed her. I hoped for her sake, the baker's price wouldn't climb any higher.

The baker grinned at me in welcome and held the door open, but I stopped a few feet away, reached into my bag, and offered him a carrot for inspection. From the corner of my eye, I watched the Coalre family walk away.

"Come now, Benella. There's no reason to do this outside. Come in."

"I'd rather not. Are you interested in trading carrots for bread, today?" I asked bluntly.

"We've enough carrots. Perhaps we can come to some other arrangement."

Swallowing a gag, I took a moment before answering.

"I think not." I placed the carrot back into the bag and turned to leave with the hope that both Tennen and Splane would be well away already.

"Benella," the baker said. "I've always thought you a pretty thing. My mother commented the other day on how pleasant you are to talk to and reminded me of my very unwed status. Perhaps, it's time to change that."

I ran and didn't look back.

I caught up with Father on the path to our cottage. At the sound of my thumping feet, he turned with a smile on his face.

"Anything interesting from the estate today?"

I slowed to walk beside him, heart hammering and stomach heavy. How could the baker even hint at marriage? The thought of his heavy body pressed against mine sickened me.

"Bini, what's wrong?" Father asked, stopping. His blue, watery eyes studied me with concern, really seeing me for a change.

"The baker hinted at marriage."

"Ah..." he said enigmatically. "And that upset you?"

"Yes. I know I won't be able to live with you forever,

but I would choose a man I could care for. One that wouldn't smother me in my sleep with his girth."

"Bini," he chided.

"He's not a good man, Father," I said firmly, hoping he would understand.

"Then, don't take his hint seriously."

Having his support calmed me. We walked the rest of the way home in silence. Bryn had no supper waiting when we returned home.

"No bread?" she asked. I shook my head and handed her the carrots.

"No worries, dears," Father assured us. "I wasn't hungry, anyway." He drifted to his study, leaving me to face Bryn's frown.

"Did you even ask?"

"Yes. He was quite clear that he wasn't interested in trading for carrots. I told you, I only have luck with his mother." I didn't like her tone, especially when I knew she had coin hidden aside that could have bought the bread.

She sighed.

"Can you try to set traps yet today? Perhaps we could have something fresh for Father at breakfast, then."

For Father, I nodded and headed back out toward the mist-filled woods. The sun hung low in the sky, sending the already dusky woods into further shadow. The dark didn't bother me. I set a few traps and walked toward the break in the estate's wall, hoping for some type of bounty. The ground sat barren, the same as it had for the last several days.

While staring dejectedly at the brown patch of dirt, I heard a faint scuffing sound behind me and turned in time to see Tennen step out from behind a tree. He held a thick segment of a broken branch. The determination in his gaze told me I wouldn't go home without injury this time.

Pivoting, I thought to run away, but Splane stepped out from behind another tree, effectively blocking the route. The hole in the wall mocked me. It was the only open path, but I knew what waited if I dared take it. No matter what I chose, I'd return home with bruises and most likely something broken.

"What did I ever do to you?" I asked Tennen, who I viewed as the bigger threat.

Instead of answering, he rushed toward me with the branch raised. I waited on the balls of my feet until the last second, then ducked under his swing in an attempt to get behind him so I could run. The movement hadn't been deep enough though because the branch raked my back. I hissed in pain, but kept moving. The gate loomed ahead, but I knew I dared not enter. I tried veering to the left toward the village, but Splane threw his rock and hit my left shoulder, effectively driving me toward the entrance. Defeated, I acknowledged they meant to corral me into the estate and darted toward the gaping black iron gate.

They chased after me, panting heavily in their exertion

to catch up. As soon as I cleared the opening, the gate slammed shut of its own accord, the clang of the metal sounding my doom.

Skidding to a stop, I spun to stare at their disdainful faces a distance from the iron bars. They weren't stupid. The bars didn't guarantee their safety. The beast had been known to venture out on occasion.

Splane saluted me in farewell and took off running. Tennen waited, watching me. When his eyes widened and the color drained from his face, I knew the beast had arrived. I watched Tennen spin and sprint away then hung my head in defeat. My back burned and shoulder ached. Had I a choice, I wouldn't have run through the gate. I had known it would only add to my hurts.

"I'm sorry," I whispered.

Behind me, the beast's growl clicked with his anger. I kept my eyes on the overgrown gravel path at my feet. I didn't try to beg or flee. It hadn't ever ended well for those who'd attempted such methods before me. Better to just accept the punishment quietly.

His growl grew louder as he crept closer, and his breath skimmed my back. Tennen, the bastard, had ripped my shirt with his vicious swing.

Something warm and wet touched my abraded skin, eliciting an involuntary hiss from my lips and a quick step forward. The growl intensified, and I froze. Had the beast just licked me?

In all of the stories told of the estate, I'd never heard any where the beast devoured trespassers. Fear of just that locked me in place, and he stepped forward and repeated his stroke. The slow drag of his tongue hurt as much as it soothed.

Several times, he covered the area from mid-back to left shoulder. The fabric of my shirt ripped further as he forced it aside with his face. I didn't move or make any further sound. With each stroke of his tongue, the pain of the scratch faded as did the throb in my shoulder where the stone had hit.

One moment he licked my skin and the next I sailed through the air, somersaulting only to land gently in a pile of hay. Coughing at the plume of dust my landing had stirred, I waved my hand in front of my face and looked at the empty place just inside the gate.

For whatever reason, the beast had spared me.

BRYN GASPED when I walked through the door. I knew I looked a mess but thought the gasp a bit of an overreaction. She hadn't even seen the back of me, yet. Blye, hearing our sister, stepped out from our room just as Bryn asked what had happened to me. Knowing Bryn wouldn't want to hear of Tennen's attack, I opened my mouth, ready to tell her that I had run into a branch. But,

Father stepped out of his study. I snapped my mouth closed.

At that moment, I loved and hated my family because of the tangled web of lies that held my tongue. Bryn hoarded Father's coin in hopes of attracting Tennen's "wealthy" hand, Blye hoarded coin to run away to a town with more prospects, and I had no doubt our intelligent Father knew of both their activities but said nothing because he was content in this poor village. All of which put pressure on me to scrounge the countryside for food and trade with that pig of a baker.

I refused to add to the lies. My anger couldn't last, though, as I watched my father's eyes soften. They were my family, all that I had.

"Well, Bini?" Father asked. "What happened to you, dear?"

"I'd rather not talk about it," I said sullenly.

"Come into my study."

Without a choice, I followed him and listened to another gasp as my sisters saw the damage to my coarse cotton shirt. I'd be forced to wear my dress tomorrow, and that annoyed me.

Father held the door for me and shut it with a soft click after I entered. I stood facing his desk while he circled around me, clucking his tongue. Behind me, he lightly touched my back where Tennen's branch had ripped into my skin.

"Looks like something scraped you, hard. Luckily, it didn't break the skin. A branch, perhaps?"

He circled around me once more to sit in his chair, studying me as he moved. I kept my face relaxed, even though I fought a growing tension. The branch had cut me, I knew it had, but somehow father only saw a scrape. The only explanation I could form was the beast's tongue. Had he really healed me? If so, to what purpose? And why throw me into the hay on my second trespass? Everyone knew that being caught a second time meant some kind of injury.

"Tennen swung a branch at me, and Splane threw a rock while I was setting traps near the estate," I said, speaking the truth.

"Why would Tennen do such a thing? I thought he liked your sister."

I snorted softly before I could stop myself and glanced at the door. Father rose quietly and peered out the door. I caught a glimpse of Blye's skirt as she turned the corner to our room.

He shut the door and raised a brow at me, encouraging me to speak.

"I saw something I wish I wouldn't have. The baker is trading for bread, but has no interest in produce. He...wanted something from Sara." A flush crept into my cheeks, and I couldn't say more.

"I see," my father murmured in surprise. "And Tennen?"

"When I fled from the baker's alley, Tennen and Splane were there, waiting for Sara. They knew I saw something I shouldn't have, and they have been making my life difficult since. They said I think I'm better than them." I met my father's eyes earnestly. "I've never knowingly given them cause to think that. We're just as poor as the rest thanks to Bryn's stealing and Blye's hoarding."

He didn't act surprised by what I said. Instead, he seemed saddened, and I knew then that I had been right. Father was aware of both my sisters' activities.

"I'm sorry you are the one to suffer for our failings. I can begrudge neither Blye keeping the coin that she works so hard to earn, nor Bryn the coin she sets aside since she keeps my house. I only regret there is nothing I can give you for your care of us."

He looked away to stare out the window for several long moments while I squirmed under my guilt for thinking poorly of him. Of course, he knew what went on in his house. I should have trusted he had a reason to allow it.

"Perhaps there is something I can do for you, now," he said. "Blye. Bryn," he called loudly, startling me. He never raised his voice.

The door opened moments later, and they crowded

into the study with us. I wondered how much my sisters had heard.

"Bryn, your sister has suffered some injuries that require a hot soak. I know it is an effort, but—"

Bryn waved away the rest of what he would say.

"I'll ready a bath for her." She turned and left.

"Blye, your sister has so little in the way of clothes and cannot afford to lose a shirt. Can you mend it?"

Blye stepped behind me, tisking. "I could, but she'll look like a beggar. Better to take the shirt apart and use some of my spare cloth for a new back panel."

"How long will that take?" Father asked.

"I should have it done tomorrow evening."

He thanked her and waved her away before turning back to me.

"Go clean up and let your sister have your shirt. Tomorrow you'll have to suffer your dress." He gave me a small grin, knowing I preferred my trousers. "The day after, I will have an errand for you, so do not make any plans for that day." He stood and planted a kiss atop my head.

Knowing I was dismissed, I stood and left his study to find a waiting Blye. She didn't look angry, so I didn't think she'd heard the part about her hoarding her coin.

"Bryn's heating water in the kitchen. Could I have your shirt? I'd like to wash it before working with it."

I didn't blame her for wanting it clean. Tracked with

dirt and beast spit, it didn't look pleasant. Since Father stayed in his study to assure privacy our small cottage lacked when any of us bathed, I quickly shrugged out of the shirt and torn bindings and handed everything over to her. She walked through the kitchen and out the back door to the well. Naked from the waist up, I covered myself with my arms and went to the kitchen.

The skin of my back felt tight, and my shoulder still ached a bit when I stretched it forward. The beast had healed me but not completely. As I sat on a chair and waited, I wondered again the reason behind his mercy. Thinking of the puzzling beast was much more pleasant than the baker's depravity or my sisters' deceit. Yet, my thoughts tended to wander in their direction.

Bryn had the fire stoked to heat the water, so I was comfortable while she sweated. A while later, she pronounced the tub ready and moved the bathing screen in front of it before stepping outside to cool herself.

I stripped down and slid into the water with a contented sigh, putting thoughts of the baker, the beast, village boys, and family lies from my head.

CHAPTER THREE

In the morning, I was last from bed, not wanting my sisters around when I dressed. Blye had thoughtfully hung my dress the night before so the wrinkles from storage would fall out on their own.

The dress was a gift from Blye and my father for my birthday more than six months ago. Father had supplied the material, and Blye had worked on it for weeks, making me stand for several painfully boring fittings. I typically only wore it on washdays and then hid in the cottage with it. Blye usually laughed at me.

Light blue with a full skirt edged with a white ruffle, topped with a square-necked, long-sleeved bodice, it truly was a thing of beauty, but I looked so different in it. I didn't think it made me look awful, just overly feminine. Secretly, I was concerned with the responsibilities wearing such a dress might bring. With my britches, most people let me go my way. Sighing, I stood and slipped the pretty dress over my head, not bothering with any bindings.

Medium height with my mother's dark sable hair and hazel eyes and my father's slim build, I looked a gangly youth in my britches and shirt. Now, the dress removed the gangle and turned me into a slender young woman. I knew that was what I was, but I didn't like it. The dress also shoved my small breasts high as if I wanted to put them on display, like produce at a market. The errant thought of selling them led to thoughts of Sara and the baker, and I decided that hiding in my room all day really was the best option.

A knock sounded on my bedroom door as I nervously smoothed my hands over the skirt. Only Father knocked, so I called for him to enter.

"You look lovely, Bini," he said with a caring smile. "I know you would prefer to stay inside, but would you walk with Bryn to the candle maker? I need another candle."

Father read by the light of the fire in his study most nights, but needed the candle for any writing he might do at his desk.

I nodded my assent and accepted the copper he handed me.

"Get the best you can with that." We both knew it wouldn't be much, but neither of us spoke it, just as I didn't question why Bryn couldn't go alone.

The candle maker had taken a dislike to Bryn a few

years before. She'd gone to purchase candles from him, and the encounter had gone badly. He'd set his price and wouldn't come down from it. She'd called him a miserly old man, which he was, but he was also nice and didn't like being called names. Regardless, she'd only gotten angry because she was a miserly young woman trying to pinch a copper whenever she could for her own selfish purpose. I didn't see how she could fault the candle maker for doing the same.

At least, by having Bryn accompany me, Father had given me the safety I needed to go about in my confounded dress. If I met up with Tennen and Splane alone while wearing it, I'd never stand a chance at outrunning them.

After lacing up my sturdy boots hidden beneath my skirts, I straightened my shoulders and headed to the kitchen. Bryn waited by the door and wore her best dress. She'd been blessed with Father's fair hair and pale eyes and our mother's curvy figure. Seeing her, I shored my resolve to ignore the stares the pair of us would receive. I knew everyone would compare us and didn't want to contemplate who would come ahead in the comparison.

"I think you've grown, Benella," Bryn commented, eyeing me dispassionately.

I quickly looked down at my skirts, which still hovered an inch above the floor.

"Not in height," she laughed as she turned away to open the door.

Refusing to think on her comment, I followed her out into the sunlight, feeling awkward as the skirts brushed against my bare legs. I didn't own any stockings, just socks and boots fit for a young boy.

"I hope Father gave you coin. I have none to spare for the candle maker," she said as I closed the door and rushed to catch up with her.

"Not enough, but the candle maker is nice, so I'm sure we can come to an agreement."

Bryn had no reply.

We walked the rest of the way to town, each lost in our own thoughts, mine mostly fervent wishes not to run into Tennen with Bryn at my side. My wishes didn't go unheard. The anvil laid quiet and the billows lax when we left the path for the main road. Relieved, I crossed the street and entered the candle maker's home. The soft chime of the bell attached to the door greeted me.

"Benella!" the candle maker exclaimed, welcoming me with a smile.

Sitting at a table near his hearth, he removed a line of strings from a pot of melted wax and set it on the holder to the side. He had once explained that his candles were the best around because he took care to ensure the candles stood straight the entire time, thus burned their wax evenly.

"What brings you in today?" he asked, standing. His bones creaked and cracked with the effort, but I didn't try to insist that he sit for our discussion. He held a firm belief that he honored his customers by standing to wait on them. His gnarled hand patted down his wispy white hair as he slowly straightened his frame.

I held out the copper.

"Father sent me for a candle. I know you offer nothing but the finest, but he'd like something modest if possible."

"Benella, your honeyed words are a trap for an unwary man, to be sure." He grinned at me, laughing and mumbling "nothing but the finest" under his breath. He didn't take the proffered coin, rather he walked to the shelves and rummaged through the pale candles for a moment before pulling out a thick one with a satisfied sigh. A blackened wick poked from one melted end.

"This is one I made for myself," he said, handing it to me. "A gift for the flowers, until I can pay you properly. Tell your father it will burn at least ten hours if he trims it."

I nodded my thanks, accepted the candle, and curled my fingers around the copper.

As I left, I debated about the coin. If I gave it to Father, he'd most likely give it to Bryn for supplies, which we wouldn't see. But, with Bryn at my side and a copper in hand, I could go to the bakery, avoid the baker, and buy some flour. After all, a copper wasn't enough to buy a loaf of bread these days.

Bryn waited for me outside. I handed her the candle, and she placed it in her bag without comment.

"I'd like to go to the bakery and see how much flour I can purchase," I said, stopping her when she would have turned home. She raised her brows at me, no doubt surprised by my willingness to linger in town when wearing a dress, and followed me without comment.

The door to the bakery stood propped open and waves of heat rolled out. No one lingered within to trade gossip today. I stepped onto the porch and quickly ducked inside the store. Miss Medunge sat on a stool behind a counter lined with a narrow variety of fresh bread. She smiled at me and waved me in.

"The bread's been picked over already. This is what's left until dinner," she said, pointing to the loaves.

"I'm interested in purchasing flour, however much a copper will get me," I said, setting the coin on the counter. I could almost taste the biscuits I imagined Bryn would make.

She pursed her lips in thought. "Just under two handfuls, I think. Do you have a bit of cloth for it?"

I cringed. "I hadn't thought of that."

"Don't worry. I can loan that if you promise to bring it back."

Nodding my promise, I watched her go through the door to the bakery. The aroma of fresh bread made my mouth water as I waited. When the door swung open, I looked up expecting her smiling face but, instead, met the eyes of the baker. In his hand, he held a small bundle of cloth tied with a bit of string.

"Benella, I couldn't believe it when my sister told me you were here to buy flour," he said while his eyes wandered over me, mostly lingering on the exposed skin of my neck and chest. "And so prettily attired. I didn't know you owned a dress."

I didn't care for his tone.

"Here is the copper," I said, scooting it across the counter with one finger.

He smirked at me and held out the flour, waiting until I reached for it to grab my fingers with his other hand. He petted them with his own sweaty digits.

"Perhaps, I will see you later," he whispered, setting the flour bag in my palm.

I said nothing, staring at him while maintaining a straight face. Eventually, he released my hand, and I turned and slowly made my exit. Sweat beaded on my upper lip when I stepped out into the cool air, but my fate didn't turn any better. Tennen stood near Bryn, and they spoke quietly. When he heard me, he looked up with a gleam in his eyes.

"Needed to see the baker?" he asked with a laugh.

Bryn, not liking that I'd immediately stolen his attention, pouted prettily, but he ignored her.

"Yes. We had a spare copper and needed flour."

A blaze of anger lit in his eyes, and he took a step

toward me. Bryn stopped him with a simpering hand on his arm.

"Tennen, our walk?"

He looked down at her, and for a moment, I saw his disdain. Then, his face cleared, and a smile curved his lips.

"Of course." He took her by the arm and led her up the road toward our house. I followed with my flour protected in my hands.

When we reached the cottage, Tennen bowed his farewell and left without looking at me again. Bryn walked inside as if nothing had happened. I handed her the flour and fled to Father's study, content to read until he returned home.

Hours melted away while I devoured the words on the pages. I'd stopped attending school years ago when I'd quietly corrected Father after class, regarding one of the mathematical concepts he'd been teaching. Since then, he let me use his study whenever he wasn't home. I remembered most everything I read that interested me, and many things did. The botany book he'd used to identify the primrose captivated me until he strode through his study door.

"What a lovely sight. A pretty girl reading a book," he said. Neither of my sisters showed much interest in books, but he didn't fault them for it.

I placed a marker in the book and set it to the side. "I've warmed your chair for you," I said cheekily.

He laughed and shooed me from the room, settling comfortably into his chair. I passed the room I shared with my sisters and saw Blye sitting on the bed, placing careful stitches into my shirt. The back panel didn't look new, just smaller. I didn't pause, not wanting to know what she had to do to fix it, and made my way to the kitchen. Bryn had the biscuits in the oven with the door slightly ajar so she could watch them brown. A knock sounded at the front door, and we stared at each other for a moment before she waved for me to answer it. I wished for my trousers as I pulled open the door.

"Benella," said the baker. "Still lovely in your dress. Is your father home? I would like to speak with him."

My legs shook. I knew the topic of conversation he wanted to have with my father but assured myself that Father understood my distaste of the man.

"Come in," I managed without a quaver. I stepped aside and let him into the kitchen.

"Wait here, please."

Leaving him to criticize Bryn's biscuits, I tapped on Father's door. Without waiting for his call to enter, I stepped in, quickly closing the door behind me.

Father looked up from his book in surprise. He still wore his jacket and simple neckcloth. Papers from his few students lay spread out on his desk.

"What is the matter, dearest?"

"He's here," I whispered in a panic. "The baker. He

saw me in this senseless dress today." I gave the skirt an agitated shake. "Now, he wants to speak with you."

"Ah," Father murmured distractedly. "Perhaps, once he's in the study with me, you'd like to go for a long stroll and forego dinner?" I nodded emphatically, liking the way Father thought. The baker, now that he had come to state his intentions, would not leave easily.

I opened the door and called to the baker. Given the size of our small cottage, he had no trouble finding me. Despite stepping aside, he still brushed against me as he passed; and this time, I couldn't suppress my shiver of revulsion. His low throaty chuckle drifted to me as I closed the door.

With a quick step, I checked on Blye's progress, hoping to change before I left, but she still sat in the room placing careful stitches. In the kitchen, Bryn removed the biscuits from the oven.

"May I have one?" I asked, grabbing my bag from the hook.

She made no comment about my leaving, just wrapped a biscuit in a cloth and handed it over. I fled the cottage quietly, hoping the baker wouldn't hear my escape.

The woods didn't feel the same as I wandered beneath their swaying limbs. The skirts encircling my legs made passage difficult. I had to avoid stretching bramble and muddied paths and made far too much noise as I moved.

When I finally reached the spot in the estate wall

where the rocks had fallen, I saw nothing to harvest. Though the walk had felt torturously long, I doubted enough time had passed to see the baker gone from the cottage. Deciding a walk in the dark didn't bother me, I turned east to make a full circuit around the wall, but a sound to the west stopped me.

A creak of wood and the crush of gravel under iron drew me toward the gate where a cart fixed with a long pole like a mast waited. The gate stood open and the cart sat just outside of it. Had someone from the estate pushed it out? What a peculiar cart. I caught sight of a tangle of freshly shorn vines laying loose at the base of the pole and felt my stomach twist. The pole, the cart, the vines...I'd seen it all before when the men had attempted to sack the estate. They'd meant to tie the beast to it and burn him. Instead, they'd been run or thrown from the estate and had abandoned the wagon, which had been later retrieved by the smith.

Turning to flee, I crashed into something solid.

"Just the person we wanted to see," Tennen murmured, clamping his hands down on my upper arms. "I thought you might run when the baker came calling."

I lifted my knee to hit his groin, but my skirts hampered the move, and I only grazed him. Still, he bent slightly, bringing his head close to mine. I jerked forward, hitting his head with my own. His hands left my arms, and I tried to run. However, the knock I'd given myself against his hard head turned me around, and I stumbled straight into Splane's waiting arms. After witnessing his brother's abuse, he quickly spun me so I faced away from him.

"Bitch!" panted Tennen, holding his nose with one hand while reaching for the vines with the other. "I hope the beast rips you open."

His sudden punch to my stomach caught me off guard. I barely noticed Splane's abandonment of his hold as the need to draw in a breath occupied me. Tennen roughly grabbed my wrists, pulled them behind my back, and tied them as I remained bent over in pain. Together the brothers hauled me onto the cart. I caught my breath enough to struggle, but it did no good. They lifted me over their heads and struggled to thread the pole through my bound arms.

"Idiots," I said when they finally stepped back, sweating and red-faced from their efforts. "You should have tied my wrists together after you had me in front of the pole."

They ignored me and jumped from the wagon. I listened to them grunt as they began to push the cart through the gates. Not again, I thought, eyeing the beast's domain.

Desperate, I leaned forward so my wrists pulled against the wood, then tried to place a foot on the pole, hoping to boost myself up and perhaps climb to the top. My heel slipped on my skirts.

"I hope the beast catches you!" I screamed at them, no longer caring if he heard the noise we were making. Oh, I still feared him but preferred he catch all of us and not just me. Perhaps I would then have a chance.

They laughed as the cart stopped moving. Facing the estate, I saw nothing but overgrown vegetation and trees. I twisted, trying to see Tennen and Splane. Instead, I heard the creak of the gate as they pulled it closed.

"We're not afraid of that thing," Tennen said, a distance behind me.

"Bold words for little men standing outside the gate," I said. "Come inside and see if you fare so well. Do your own dirty work instead of waiting for someone else to do it for you!"

"Someone? You mean something. This is the third time for you, isn't it, Benella? You won't bother us again."

Tennen spoke the truth, and I struggled against the thin vines binding my wrists. The beast would not forgive a third trespass. I wriggled and writhed and panted as I fought against my binding. Pain bit into my wrists with each frantic tug and twist, and my fingers grew slick. My hair came loose from its long braid and tangled in front of my face, obscuring my vision.

Tennen's laughter taunted me and my pathetic struggles until the sound abruptly stopped. I stilled and tried blowing the hair from my eyes. For a fraction of a moment, I caught a glimpse of black eyes and brown fur before my hair once again blocked my view. I froze. The beast. He was here, mere feet away.

The dark trees around us had gone eerily quiet as if holding their breath. The silence allowed the low rumble of the beast's growl to echo, surrounding me with his menace.

A scrape against the ground and a faint creak of the wood was all the warning I had before the beast pushed the cart and sent it flying to crash upon the gate. The bone-jarring stop rattled my teeth as my head smacked back against the pole. The momentum sent me forward again, a sudden jerk stopped by my tied wrists. The vines bit deep, and I grunted in pain.

Behind me, Splane squealed like a girl a moment before I heard their hurried retreat. I laughed groggily as my ears rang and the world spun from the thump to my head.

"Two little girls, that's what they are. They should be wearing a dress," I mumbled, wincing at the pain at the base of my skull.

"Why have you returned?" asked an angry voice in a deep scraping growl.

He could speak? With a curtain of hair in the way and my vision not cooperating, I closed my eyes in defeat.

"That should be apparent, I'd think. To die."

"Why do you wish for death so badly?" the voice

asked. Some of the anger had faded from it and was replaced by curiosity.

"Does it look to you like I came here by choice?" A harsh laugh escaped me. "It's not my wish, but theirs, that I die."

The longer I stood there, the more my injuries started calling attention to themselves. My shoulders ached from their position and the recent collision with the gate. My wrist oozed blood and my stomach twisted with nausea. His silence along with everything else made my next words dangerously impudent.

"Recent events having left me in a poor mood, I'd rather not waste any more time on idle conversation. I hurt everywhere and think I may vomit soon so, please, just be done with it."

The vines around my wrists loosened, and I fell forward onto something hard, furry, and warm. Draped over the beast, I realized, a moment before we were moving.

Sadly, I vomited before fainting.

"...SHOULD I?"

The shrill voice cut through the fog clouding my mind, and I blinked my eyes open to stare at the rough shingled roof blurring above me. A growl filled the air, and my stomach lurched, not from the growl, but from the sour taste lingering in my mouth. I gagged.

"Leave us," the feminine voice commanded.

A door slammed, and I turned on my side to dry heave. A gentle hand ran over my hair, lingering on the spot at the back of my head where I'd smacked against the pole.

"There's the problem. Let's sit you up."

She leveraged a thin, wiry arm behind my shoulders and helped me sit. Slowly, my vision cleared and an aged, haggard face filled the space before me. White hair twisted tightly behind her head and pulled the skin of her face, smoothing a few of the deeper creases. Her brilliant green eyes glinted at me with cold humor.

"Got in the way of something, I'd say," she murmured, leaning in close, her gaze shifting back and forth to study mine. "Best to stay awake tonight. You'll feel sick, which is normal. Drink lightly. Don't eat until your stomach stops twisting."

Without mercy, she tugged me to my feet. The ground tilted and heaved, and I spread my stance wide to keep from falling.

"Smart girl," she said with a laugh. "Too bad he brought you to me. You can't stay here. Out you go." She nudged me toward the door.

The stomach I'd thought empty heaved again, and I left a gift on her floor before I managed to clear the threshold. Her insulting laughter rang out behind me before the door closed and silence enveloped me.

Reaching out, I braced myself on the door. Night had claimed the sky and the half-moon weakly highlighted the area, not that it did me any good. The pain in my head clouded my vision. How would I manage a walk home, especially when I didn't know where I was? I recalled the beast's growl and knew I had to be somewhere within the estate. South, then, was the way to go. I lifted my head to the moon, trying to focus enough to get my bearings.

I took a lurching step away from the door, my skirt swishing through the grass. Within seven steps, I heaved again, and my eyes watered. The muscles in my stomach protested, and I wished for a cool drink to rinse my mouth. Instead, I received a growl.

"Vomit on me again, and you will suffer," he said before he swung me over his shoulder. The grass flew past us, and I clenched my teeth as blood rushed to my head and pulsed in my ears. My vision clouded, and I knew I'd faint again and wondered if that counted as sleeping. The beast sensed something, though, because he stopped his run, and I found myself standing before him in the shadowy light beneath a tree.

"What did she say?" he demanded.

When the world tilted, I didn't try widening my stance. Instead, I let my weak knees fold and sat heavily on the ground.

"Don't sleep or eat until my stomach stops twisting. Drink lightly and get out." I partially groaned as I struggled to my knees and heaved again, aggravating my stomach muscles and the lump on the back of my head. I spit weakly and let my head hang.

"Running upside down made it worse," I said, swiping at my lips.

"You blame this on me?" His low growl increased in volume and clicked with menace as he crept close to me.

"Well, it was your fault that I hit the back of my head against the pole. Before that, only my wrists bled."

He roared in response, which brought back the ringing in my ears. I paid his anger little mind as I sought refuge from my pain in the cool grass and closed my eyes.

"What are you doing?"

"Going to sleep."

"The witch said not to."

"And you just roared at me. So what? If I die, I die. I'm tired of being bullied by you and the idiots in the village. If I live, so be it. At least, I'll have had a few moments of peace."

His feet padded softly, rustling the grass and scraping the dirt until he stopped behind me. Lying on my side with my face cushioned by my arm, I'd saved the back of my head from touching the ground, but also left it open to the beast's inspection. He huffed a great breath, blowing my hair over my face. Then he began to lick the lump he'd made.

I couldn't help the sigh that escaped me as the ache eased and the twisting in my stomach faded.

"Thank you," I whispered.

He grunted and kept licking for several more minutes. Without the nausea, it lulled me to sleep.

CHAPTER FOUR

"CAW!"

I bolted upright at the loud cry in my ear. My stomach muscles protested at their overuse, and I suffered a brief period of disorientation. I recalled the night before and studied my surroundings. The shaded glade only sported a few tufts of low growing grass on the outskirts. A soft patch grew in the center where the sun struck at midday, the very patch on which I'd previously reclined until the crow, hopping on the ground a few feet away, had rudely woken me.

The crow cawed at me again, but I ignored it as I struggled to my feet. The aches of the night before lingered in my shoulders and stomach but remained absent elsewhere, drawing my attention to the smooth and unblemished skin of each wrist. The memory rose of how the beast had eased the ache in my head. I glanced around the glade but felt certain only the crow and I entertained it now.

Given the dangerously unpredictable nature of the beast, I thought it best to keep my company to myself, and I began to carefully pick my way through the trees, heading toward the general area of the gate. As soon as I started walking, the crow took flight only to land on a branch ahead of me. I ignored the bird for the most part since it kept quiet when it flew but listened closely to the surrounding wood as I made slow progress through the estate lands.

It didn't surprise me when I spotted the gate ahead and it grated open on its own, the estate obviously ready to be rid of me. Of the beast, there was no sign. Muddied and disheveled, I made my way home in dawn's first light.

A FAMILIAR GASP greeted me when I opened the kitchen door. Behind me, a furious flutter of wings sounded, prompting me to ignore Bryn's incredulous stare and quickly close the door before the annoying crow decided to let itself in. It cawed at me through the wood.

"Benella," Bryn finally managed to cry. "Father's been so worried." She stood by the stove with an apron wrapped around her dress. Eggs fried in a pan, and a small crock of fresh goat's milk already rested on the table, waiting for Father.

The study door opened, and Father hurried out fully dressed for the day, his expression putting truth to Bryn's statement. His eyes swept me and relief erased the worry.

"When I mentioned a walk, I didn't think you'd stay out all night, child," he said mildly, seeing me whole and healthy.

"An unplanned event to be sure," I said. "I ran into a bit of dirt and will need another bath."

Bryn gave a small, exasperated huff.

"I can't haul water for you again, Benella. I'm supposed to go with Tennen to—"

"Bryn," Father said softly. "I'm sure it wouldn't over trouble you to help with two small buckets, just enough to rinse the dirt from your sister's hair." As he spoke, he circled me and lifted the hair on the back of my head.

"Surely this unplanned event had a few interesting turns," he murmured for my ears only.

I gave the barest of nods, and he stepped back from me. I appreciated that he didn't question me further.

"At least the dress survived unscathed," he said.

Blye harrumphed from the doorway of our room. She'd joined us so quietly I hadn't noticed her.

"Its hem is stained with mud. I wouldn't call that unscathed."

"Better than ripped," Father said in a tone that didn't

allow for argument. "Benella, I would speak with you before I leave about an errand I need you to run. Would you mind stepping into my study before you wash?"

"Of course, Father," I said, more than willing to escape my sisters' pique.

He surprised me by not asking of my night once he closed the door behind us.

"I apologize for asking this of you, but I need a message delivered to the Head in Water-On-The-Bridge as soon as possible."

The request disheartened me. The walk would take me most of the day there and back, and sleeping on the ground the prior night had done little to leave me feeling rested. But, I reasoned with myself, a whole day with no other obligations might be nice. I rolled my shoulders, feeling the ache in the joints, and tested my stomach. Nothing I couldn't handle. So, I nodded my agreement. Outside the window, a crow squawked.

"Fetch your mended shirt from Blye. I'm sure you'll be more comfortable in it," he said. "See me when you're ready to leave."

I nodded and quietly crept to my room. After carefully closing the door, I looked around the room. My shirt lay neatly on the thin comforter of my narrow bed. Something about it looked odd, but I couldn't determine what when I lifted it up. As usual, Blye's stitches ran small and straight, making it impossible to see where she'd made any change. I slipped out of the dress and pulled on my trousers then bindings.

Outside, I heard a flutter of wings; and as I looked up at the partially shuttered window, the crow used his beak to make room for himself on the ledge. Blye opened the door behind me before I could shoo the crow away.

"Did you try it on?" she asked impatiently.

I turned away from the voyeuristic crow and shrugged my arms into the shirt. It fit, but it pulled snugly from shoulder to shoulder across the back. Frowning, I closed the front and began to button it up, seeing the problem immediately. The shirt buttons strained to close the gap between the front two panels and created small spaces where anyone could see my bindings or stomach for that matter.

Disappointment clearly on my face, I looked up at her. Her expression remained impassive.

"Well, I tried. The cloth I had didn't match, and you would have looked like a patchwork. Perhaps Father can save for a new one. Until then, you do have the dress."

I stared after her as she glided from the room and closed the door. The dress? In a disbelieving trance, I walked across the room to one of the compact chests sitting on the floor at the foot of the larger bed that Blye and Bryn shared. There was one chest for each of my sisters, gifts from our mother, who'd died before giving one to me. She'd meant them as a place for us to store the things we would collect for our own homes.

Carefully lifting the lid of Blye's chest, I gazed at the yards of folded fabrics stacked neatly on top of each other and the various lengths of ribbon lying on top of them. Threads of several colors twined around a thin spindle. Under the spindle, a simple bolt of roughly woven cream cotton material rested all but forgotten beside the prettily colored fine weaves. I would have liked to think Blye had overlooked the material; but wrapped in a bit of coarse thread, the section on my shirt she'd taken away sat beside it. She was right. The colors didn't quite match, but she had enough of the other material to make me a whole new shirt if she chose to. It hurt knowing she couldn't spare anything for me when I'd given so much to her.

A clicking at the window distracted me; and I let the lid close softly, leaving the contents undisturbed. The crow opened and closed its beak several times without making any other sound and then took off from the sill, leaving me in peace.

Shaking out the dress and brushing as much of the dirt from it as I could, I spread it on the bed and went to the kitchen to wash up. Two kettles rested on the stove in the vacant kitchen. I fetched a cloth and tested the water. Still cool. Frowning, I checked the stove. Bryn hadn't even added wood to it to heat the water. Sighing, I set to washing in the cold water, wiping my skin, but foregoing rinsing my hair. Instead, after I finished and changed back into the dress, I ran a brush through it then braided it again.

Tossing the water into the garden out back, I noticed the crow watching from the top of our tiny outbuilding that housed the goat and a few garden tools. It watched me closely, its quiet more disturbing than its previous cawing. I thoughtfully narrowed my eyes at it before going inside.

Finally ready, I knocked on Father's study door. He stood before the window, staring out at nothing when I entered, but quickly turned to hand me a sealed letter.

"Try to be home before dark and save me from another night's worry, Bini," he said softly, kissing my cheek.

I nodded and moved aside to let him pass. He'd obviously been waiting for me so he could leave for the school and ring the bell to call his pupils.

THE CROW FOLLOWED me as I walked away from the cottage, heading northwest toward the road. I wanted to angle north enough to miss any possibility of running into Tennen or Splane. I imagined by now, Tennen knew I'd returned home, thanks to Bryn, and wondered at his reaction.

Lost in thought, I continued my journey until the crow flew at me from the left, making a racket and flapping in my face. Raising my arms for protection, I turned away, instinctively taking several large steps to put distance between us. So far, the crow had just followed me; the violence of its sudden attack left me with a racing heart and confused. I had no food with me to give it cause to chase me, even though the journey promised to be long and tiring.

It retreated, and I tentatively lowered my arms to look for it. It had perched on a branch not far to my left. It cocked its head, studying me intensely. Warily, I gave it wide berth and tried striking out northwest again. Every time I veered even the slightest bit in a westerly direction, it flew at me.

Scowling, I headed north to the estate. It followed me closely, herding me to the gate, which swung open at my approach. I stopped to look at the crow.

"I truly feel I've tempted fate enough. I don't suppose you'd leave me in peace if I went no further."

It cawed angrily, and I sighed, eyeing its sharp beak. Hoping the beast's benevolent mood remained intact in the light of day, I stepped through the gate. As soon as it slammed closed behind me, the crow flew off north toward the center of the estate. Nervously, I lingered by the gate, unwilling to risk increasing the beast's ire by going any further.

After several long minutes the small, unidentifiable noises made by the wildlife in the surrounding area quieted. The typically blurred air grew murkier, making it hard to see more than a few feet beyond where I stood. A caw sounded nearby, the sharp ring of it dampened by the mist.

"You returned." The beast's disembodied growl floated to me.

Standing my ground, I slowly scanned the darkest areas in front of me.

"Not by choice. I think your crow would have eagerly pecked out my eyes had I not abided by its direction."

Silence answered me. Had I misunderstood? Was the crow not his messenger? My stomach churned, and my gaze darted from one shadowy object to the next as I tried to discern which might be the beast. After a few moments of straining to see or hear any indication I wasn't alone, I bravely spoke.

"I'm very willing to leave you to your peace if you would kindly convince the gate to open."

"Before you leave, you may ask of me one thing you need that I can find within the walls of my estate," he said with a low rumble.

My mouth popped open. Generosity from the beast was the last thing I'd expected.

"I...thank you for your offer," I said slowly, "but I've taken so much from the estate already."

"You scorn my offer?"

The roar of his rage momentarily deafened me and

startled nearby birds from their roosts. Rubbing my ears, I hastily tried to assure him.

"Never scorn. To the east, a portion of your wall has crumbled and often the area beyond offers a small harvest of edible roots no matter what time of year. Many times it's helped feed me. And just the other day, a spider threw its fine webbing at me, strong enough to use as thread. To my shame, I've never scorned the bounty of your estate. I've repeatedly taken without asking until finally it stopped offering. So you see, I can't possibly accept more."

An annoyed grunt sounded to my right, but when I turned in that direction, I saw nothing.

"Regardless, ask of me one thing you need. Only then will the gate open."

I frowned at his stubborn insistence. Why did I need to ask for something? Perhaps it was a trick, and if I asked for the wrong thing I'd be trapped in the estate forever. He'd said something in the estate that I needed. Need must be the key. If Blye stood before him, she would say she needed something silly like thread or material, but I knew neither could be a need.

"I can think of nothing I need. We always have enough food to keep from starving and a roof to keep us warm and dry."

"I don't care about your family," he said sharply. "Whatever you choose must be for you and you alone. You waste my time. This is no riddle to debate and stew. Just choose," he bellowed, causing me to jump.

Thoughtfully quiet, I nibbled at my lip. It was on the tip of my tongue to ask for a man's shirt. I even opened my mouth and made a small noise before snapping it shut as a surprising thought stopped me. I could hear his growing agitation in the increased volume of his growl.

"Refuge," I whispered.

The growling stopped.

"What do you mean?"

"You want me to ask for one thing I need from within the estate. I'm asking for refuge when I need it."

Behind me, the gate creaked open. I spun and raced for the breach, not waiting for his answer. The crow's cackling caw followed me through the trees until I reached the point where the mists faded.

Near the road, I paused to bend and catch my breath. Four times I'd stood within the walls of the estate and escaped with my life; and now, with his offer, I'd ensured my safety if I should ever find myself within those walls again.

After a few moments, I wiped away the sweat that had accumulated on my brow and started my journey. The letter from my father rested within the bag that lay limp against my hip. I wished I had something with which to carry water, for I sorely needed a drink and my journey had just begun.

Recalling Father's request to return before dark, I lengthened my stride and followed the road from the estate northwest.

THE ROAR of rushing water announced the Deliichan River, which bordered the hilltop village of Water-On-The-Bridge. Eager to deliver the message, I strode forward around the last bend in the road and caught my first glimpse of the water-slicked bridge. In winter, the spray from the water that crashed upon the rocks below froze on the thick, wood planks to create a treacherous trek across.

For as long as anyone could remember, there had always been water on the bridge, the reason for the village's name. They'd tried moving the bridge, but the river didn't tolerate additional bridges well, and they usually fell to ruin shortly after their completion. Only this one remained steadfast with very little repair needed.

Because of the precariousness of the bridge, many merchants ended their routes at Water-On-The-Bridge, not bothering to trade with Konrall. The baker made the journey once a month for his flour from the mill while the tinker only rode this way when his supplies ran low. The seamstress and the candle maker dealt with the single traveling merchant who still traversed the bridge.

My footsteps echoed hollowly on the planks and fine

droplets settled on my cheeks as I crossed. The mill stood as a tall sentinel on the opposite side of the river, its elevated floors hovering a few feet above the water, steady on the thick stilts sunk deep into the riverbed. The waterwheel that turned the stone grinder spun slowly in the swift current, but I knew its power and the fine powder it turned out.

The road on the other side of the river suffered deep ruts due to the constant traffic from the town to the mill. I took care to traverse the shoulder so I could view the bustling trade without fear of being run down by horse or wagon. There was much to observe.

Water-On-The-Bridge presented a larger variety of trade than Konrall, including things a proper lady shouldn't stare at. However, without my father accompanying me, I took the opportunity to watch the alehouse women, whom I knew if asked, would serve more than a drink.

A tall brunette laughed loudly, throwing her head back to expose her neck. It made her look pretty, smoothing the lines of her loose skin and bringing a natural flush to her mottled complexion. Her customer, a man at ease while he sipped ale at a table, watched her chest with interest. Her dress pushed the tops of her pale breasts up on display much as my dress did. The man reached forward and pulled her close with a tug on her skirt. She leaned down to hear what he said, and he buried his face in her cleavage. She laughed harder as I passed from their view.

The scene made me distinctly uncomfortable with my own display, but I persisted forward, knowing the house I sought was highly respectable. Mr. Jolen Pactel, the current Head, lived past the House of Whispering Sisters, which I found entertaining since his purpose was to maintain the peace and theirs was to bring peace, but in completely different ways. As Head, Mr. Pactel settled disputes and set down judgments in place of the Liege Lord, an absent fellow for near fifty years. The title of Head wasn't an elected one, but an inherited one; and the Pactel family had held the position of Head for the last forty years with fair rulings. The House of Whispering Sisters brought peace, one client at a time, with their sweet smelling smoke, veiled faces, and unveiled bodies.

With nothing to trade and no coin, I suffered the delicious aromas of simmering stews and baking pastries as I walked through the market district. The cloying smoke from the Whispering Sisters house fogged my head briefly as I caught a glimpse of a pale, slim torso and a grey veiled face through an open window.

Away from the noise of commerce, I stepped under the arched stone wall that bordered the two-story house of the Head. After a single knock, the dense oak door swung open, and a thick-armed man greeted me with an impassive look.

"Good day. I have a message for the Head from Mr. Benard Hovtel of Konrall."

The man stepped aside and bid me to enter. I willingly stepped into the spacious entry and admired the smooth sanded plank floor covered with a pretty, woven rug. Spring flowers adorned the side table, scenting the air sweetly.

"This way," the man murmured, leading me toward a small room near the back of the house.

A smaller man sat behind a desk there. Sitting in a chair in the corner near the door through which we walked was another thick-armed man. I understood the business of the Head and knew men strong enough to help keep the peace were needed.

"She has a message for the Head," the man announced behind me once I entered the room. Without waiting for a response from the man behind the desk, my escort left.

The short, thin man at the desk looked up from his papers, and with a pleasant smile, he stood when he saw me.

"Good day, dear lady," he greeted me. "Mr. Pactel is currently occupied elsewhere in the Water. May I be of assistance?"

"I'm not certain," I said hesitantly. "My father sent me here to deliver this message to Mr. Pactel." I reached into my bag, heard the man in the corner shift behind me, and quickly withdrew the sealed letter. When I glanced over my shoulder, the man was just settling back into his chair, eyeing me critically.

"And you are?"

"Sorry," I said, remembering myself. "Benella."

"I am Tibit. Would you mind if I read the letter?" He didn't reach for the letter I held out, letting me decide first. Since I had no idea what it contained, I didn't know what to say. Though my father trusted me, at least I thought he did, he knew to what extent I could protect his letter and surely wouldn't write anything of significant importance.

"I think that would be fine, Mr. Tibit."

"Just Tibit will do," he said politely, reaching for the letter. He broke the seal and scanned the contents. "Ah, yes. The school master."

"My father," I clarified.

Tibit looked up at me with a half-smile.

"Tell your father the offer still stands, and we are pleased to hear he is finally considering it."

With that, he moved back to his desk, effectively dismissing me with not one offer of refreshment or further explanation. I kept my disappointment from my face and thanked him for his time before taking my leave. A hint about the offer after which my father had inquired would have been nice, but a drink much more welcomed.

AFTER SOME TIME on the road, the rattle and clink of a wagon sounded ahead. Cautiously, I moved aside. Traffic from Konrall was rare, and I wasn't sure what to expect. Perhaps the baker was heading toward the mill for his flour. I quickly fled the road. The mist welcomed me as I slipped through the trees in the direction of the wall. The rattle of the wagon grew louder as it neared.

Peeking through the trees, I sighed in relief when I spotted the traveling merchant's wagon but didn't step out to greet him. I didn't want to startle the horses. Exhausted, I trudged the rest of the way home to arrive before dinner and Father's return.

"Where did Father send you?" Bryn asked, opening the cottage door before I could knock.

"Please, sister," I said. "I'm tired, thirsty, and hungry. Let me in so I can sit."

She scowled at me but moved aside so I could shuffle into the dim cottage. The sky had grown increasingly dark during my journey home, and now a thick, light grey blanket of clouds covered the sun. With no candles to spare, Bryn had lit a fire in the hearth to try to brighten the kitchen. I sat in a chair and sighed when she sat across from me.

"Well?"

It wasn't that I expected my sister to wait on me. I'd just thought she would have the courtesy to offer to get me a drink after knowing I'd been gone all day. Tiredly, I stood and fetched myself a cup of water.

"Benella. Really, where are your manners? I'm asking you a question," she said.

"Water-On-The-Bridge," I managed to say between gulps.

"How unfair," Bryn cried.

Blye stepped into the room from our bedroom, two panels of fabric in her hands and pins in her mouth. Bryn spotted the question in her eyes and explained.

"Father sent Benella to Water-On-The-Bridge." Bryn turned back to me. "We're both older. We should have been allowed to go."

I set down the cup with a laugh.

"You would have walked twelve miles and back in a single day without any food or water? I doubt not."

Bryn had the decency to look slightly embarrassed. "I thought Father sent you in a wagon."

"With what coin?" I said, exasperated. Her face took on a flushed hue, and Blye's eyes rounded. "I'm tired," I said quickly before she could respond. I turned to head to our room.

Blye spit the pins out into one of her hands.

"You can't go in there. I'm using your bed to lay out my dress pattern." I stared at her. Using my bed to make another new dress for herself? Perhaps, if I hadn't been so tired, my temper would have sparked, but I couldn't find the energy.

Instead of answering, I turned and let myself into Father's study, closing the door behind me. His chair wasn't very comfortable to sleep in, but the rug before his hearth would suit me fine. I lay down on the floor and closed my eyes.

CHAPTER FIVE

"Bini, child, wake up," Father said softly, touching my hair.

The shoulder pressing into the rug ached with cold, and my eyes felt hot and gritty as I blinked them open. Outside, the wind blew, rattling the branches, and a slight breeze came down the unlit chimney in Father's study.

"Come eat some warm soup," he encouraged, helping me to my feet.

In the kitchen, Bryn and Blye waited at the table. The unusual sight gave me pause. They never held dinner for me. As soon as I sat, Bryn started serving a thick vegetable soup.

"I assume everything went well at the Water, Bini?" Father asked while we waited.

"The Head was absent, but Tibit said they were pleased you were considering their offer."

"What offer?" Blye inquired.

"A private teaching position."

Bryn paused in her ladling.

"That's the one you considered before we moved here, isn't it? Four years is a long time for a position to remain open. What's wrong with it?"

"The position is fine. The pay is slightly more than I make now," he assured us.

I watched my sisters' eyes glimmer with excitement, but I felt wary.

"Why didn't you take it four years ago, then?" I asked.

Bryn passed the soup around. It filled the void in my stomach and warmed my blood.

He gave me a slight, sad smile.

"The cottage is not fit for a family of four." Before my sisters could ask how he meant for us to live there if there wasn't enough room for all of us, he added, "But now you are of an age to marry."

Blye clapped her hands with a huge smile.

"You've accepted the baker's request for Benella, then?"

My stomach dropped, and the soup I'd recently eaten soured in it. Surely, he wouldn't force me to wed the Baker after what I'd told him.

"Benella is still too young to wed, just as you were too young in my mind four years ago."

Blye's face turned to stone. "Surely, you don't expect one of us to wed the baker."

"I will not force a groom onto you if you have no care for him. That said, are there any you care for?"

"I'd accept Tennen if he asked," Bryn said demurely.

"I'm afraid that match wouldn't suit you, dearest. The Coalre family is as out of coin as the rest of us, and I would not have you going into a marriage with false ideas or hopes," he said calmly between sips of broth.

I stayed focused on my own meal, but from the corner of my eye saw my sister's face flush at Father's blunt words. Part of me wanted to cheer him in his softly worded criticism of her shallow nature, but I squelched that part, knowing it unkind to Bryn. As Father stated, she did work hard, most of the time, to keep the cottage a home. What would happen when she and Blye both wed? Who would mend for Father and cook for him? I could do a fair job at a meal if a person didn't mind a lack of variety. Mending bored me to tears, but I could sew a straight line. I'd never have the skill of either Bryn or Blye, though. Unless my future husband was a tailor, I didn't see that my lack of skill would matter.

"If you have no preferences, I'd like to announce your intent to marry and see what offers we receive," Father said into the silence.

"How soon?" Bryn whispered.

"In the morning, I'll talk to the baker. By evening, the rest of the village should know."

A FLAT-FACED SHEEP farmer from the south came to offer for Blye after Father returned home. The short, muscled man spoke plainly of his need for someone who could weave and sew well and promised himself to be a soft-spoken, gentle man. Given his propensity to gaze at the ground when speaking to Blye instead of meeting her gaze, I agreed with his self-assessment. After listening to his offer, Blye kindly declined.

Bryn consoled Blye after the man left, saying at least someone had come for her. Though Father had discounted Tennen, I felt sure Bryn still held out some small hope that he would appear and offer for her nonetheless. She quietly served another dinner of vegetable soup; and I knew, dress or no, I needed to attempt to set traps the following day.

I CREPT from bed during the twilight hour when the birds sang gustily before the dawn. Shaking out my dress, I frowned at its dingy, pale blue color. It needed a washing desperately, but I put it on anyway and hustled out the door before Father rose from bed. The cool air prickled my skin; and I set out toward the estate, carefully placing traps on my way, to check the enchanted dirt that spilled from the wall.

When I reached the rough patch of soil, I wasn't disappointed by barren earth. A single line of turnips thinly dotted the expanse, starting from the edge to lead toward the tumbled rock. The row didn't stop there but continued with uprooted turnips lying on their sides over the rocks and into the darkened woods within, a blatant invitation that struck me as very wrong. I stared at the roots while biting on my lower lip. My stomach growled. I wanted the food, no doubt about it, but I wasn't willing to fall into some sort of trap, which was how it appeared to me. I recalled all of the other times I'd harvested there and walked the boundary, looking to pluck any bounty I could find.

Rifling through my bag, my hand clasped around a spare ribbon I used to tie back my hair. The color had faded and the ends were frayed, but I laid it down on the ground anyway.

"It's not much, but all I have," I whispered, "for the things I've taken in the past. Thank you."

Before I changed my mind, or my hunger changed it for me, I darted away. Behind me, I heard the vines moving and ran faster, hoping the estate wouldn't hold a grudge over everything I'd taken. It was the only explanation I had for its odd behavior.

I should have known I couldn't outrun magic. The vines flew along the ground and caught me by the ankles while others stretched down from lofty heights within the canopy to curl around my upper arms and lift me high.

"Please," I whispered as they shuffled me back toward the wall. "I meant no offense."

Ahead I saw the turnip filled dirt and crumbling wall. The vines didn't set me down there. They kept shuffling me forward over the wall and through the dark misty trees as the sky began to lighten. Finally, before a large gnarled oak growing at the edge of a pond, they released me. I landed with a splash in the waist-deep waters and scowled. Dripping wet, I stood weighed down by my heavy skirts.

"Confounded dress," I muttered, struggling toward the shore.

The tree groaned, a low noise of wood rubbing on wood, then gave several small splintering cracks as the surface of the trunk began to shift. I stopped my approach and stood still in the knee-deep water to watch with wide eyes as a face formed within the wood. Rough, slashed bark eyes squinted at me, and a great long nose twitched as if the eyes couldn't believe what they saw. Below the nose a wide mouth opened slowly, looking as if the tree was breaking and about to topple. Instead, it spoke.

"Teach him," it said in a series of cracks and groans. The leaves above trembled with its effort.

"Who?" I whispered, fear and awe having stolen the volume from my voice.

"Free us," it continued as if it didn't hear me. The trunk tilted forward again as the mouth closed and the nose sank back into the bark, leaving only the slitted eyes until they too winked out of existence.

Looking around at the woods, I waited for more, but nothing else happened for several long minutes. Shivering, I climbed out of the water and walked back toward the wall. This time, I took the turnips, every one of them.

From the traps, I managed to gather two rabbits, which pleased me until I wondered how to skin them without dirtying my dress. After my dunking, it was clean once again. While I contemplated my dilemma, I continued home, glad to see a faint glow in the kitchen window. Bryn willingly surrendered her apron, only raising a brow at my damp state, and I set to work, eager to eat rabbit for breakfast.

Father stepped from his study as I handed over the dressed game to Bryn along with her now dirty apron.

"Father, do you know of the estate's history?" I asked, ignoring Bryn's peevish glance.

He shook his head.

"Only what we know from the villagers, that the beast guards the estate for the Liege Lord to prevent theft and whatnot," he said absently, looking in our food storage for something to eat.

He was right. The information he knew was nothing I hadn't already heard. When we'd moved here, I'd been young enough that I hadn't cared about the beast or the estate beyond the need to stay away from them. However, since both the estate and the beast seemed to have taken an interest in me, I needed to learn more.

"I'll bring some of the rabbit to the school when it's ready if you'd like," I said to him.

He nodded his thanks and left as I moved closer to the stove to dry and enjoy the scent of cooking meat. Bryn left to milk the goat and check for an egg from our single hen. In the warm silence, I contemplated which of the villagers might know more regarding either the estate or the beast. Miss Medunge, the baker's sister, loved gossiping and probably knew everything about everyone, but I didn't want to chance meeting up with the baker. The butcher hadn't lived here as long as we had, and the seamstress didn't have any interest in anything other than her cloth and customers. The Coalres were out of the question for obvious reasons. That left the candle maker.

AFTER TAKING a covered plate to Father, I cautiously hurried to the candle maker. I'd yet to face Tennen or Splane after their last attempt to have the beast kill me and wanted to keep it that way.

The candle maker's bell above the door rang as I let myself in after a brief knock. He looked up from his work with a smile.

"I hadn't thought to see you so soon," he said. "But I'm glad you're here, nonetheless. I have something for you." He stood with a grunt and shuffled to a low shelf near the back of the room. Lying on the rough board, a blunt silver glimmered in the daylight. He plucked it from the wood between two time-twisted fingers and shuffled toward me, wearing an excited grin.

"Timmy couldn't believe the primrose candle," he said, handing me the coin, which I took reluctantly. "If you find more flowers, bring them to me and there will be more silver for you," he promised.

I fisted the silver but didn't turn to go.

"I was wondering if you could tell me a little about the history of the estate. Or perhaps, something of the beast."

"It would brighten the rest of my morning to spend it telling you stories from my youth. But, come, sit. I can't forget my work while we talk."

He nudged another chair close to his worktable, and I willingly sat with him. The candle maker's cottage was always pleasantly warm. He checked his strings and started his tale.

"I was about your age when the Liege Lord disappeared, but I remember the years before that well enough to be glad of his absence. He was a man far too concerned with his own pleasures than that of the people who looked to him for protection and justice. Justice," the candle maker scoffed. "Back then it was a mockery. The Head at the Water used the position to swindle the businesses and bully the people he didn't like. The Liege Lord did nothing. He couldn't. He was too busy strutting from bed to bed, not caring what women occupied it with him."

I kept quiet, afraid he'd recall his audience and stop his open retelling.

"I shouldn't say that," he said. "He did care. Only the pretty ones. Young. Old. Single. Married. He made no distinction." He snorted disgustedly. "I'm ahead of myself. The estate has been there over three hundred years and has passed from father to son. While the last Liege Lord's father had lived, things were peaceful and prosperous. After his father died, the Liege Lord started his whoring. His mother, too ashamed of her son, retired to the South and died there not long after. The young Lord just sank deeper into his depravity. Things were getting to the point where I was thinking of heading south, too—the southern liege lords are good to their tenants—but then he disappeared. He just stopped going to the villages. Stopped his whoring. The Head went to the estate but found it empty. He thought to make himself a little coin and take a few things, and that was the first time the beast made himself known. Oh, that Head ran down the road, here, screaming something fierce. Took several men to hold him down and pour ale down his throat before he calmed enough to tell what happened. 'Course no one believed him, and a group went to the estate to see for themselves."

He cackled at the memory.

"That's when the legend of the beast really started. The Head went back to the Water, but soon came with all sorts of people interested in trying to kill the beast to get to the Liege Lord's treasure. But that beast protected it something fierce. Many men died trying to get past the gate. As time passed and the flow of would-be pillagers slowed, some folks managed to get in the gate, but never very far. I think the beast knew they were just curious for the most part and didn't harm them. But those that return for a second visit, well, he doesn't treat them as well."

"What about the Liege Lord? Where did he go?"

"Some say he went south to mourn his mother, but fifty years is a long time to mourn. No, I think he's at the estate," he said softly. "I think he never left. That beast keeps him as cornered in the estate as he does keeping folks out. I just can't figure out why."

I thanked him for his time, and at the last moment, remembering the coin curled in my fist, thanked him for that as well. He certainly had given me plenty to think on.

Leaving the candle maker, I collided with Sara, the smith's wife. I didn't pay her as much attention as I did Splane, who trailed behind her. He glared at me as I smoothed my skirt with both hands while absently apologizing to Sara. The feel of fabric against the sweaty palm that used to hold a coin froze me in place. I'd dropped it.

"Excuse me, Benella," Sara said stiffly, a deep hue of crimson flooding her face.

Did she too know what I'd witnessed? I felt horrible.

A glint in the dust at our feet caught my eyes. I looked down at it, making my notice obvious.

"I think you dropped something."

Sara's eyes followed mine and rounded. She didn't hesitate, but snatched up the blunt silver.

"We don't need your charity," Splane said mulishly.

His mother's fingers curled tightly around the coin. Easy words for him when he didn't need to spread his legs for the baker.

"Charity?" I asked, feigning puzzlement. "How would I come by a blunt silver?" I let the doubt in my voice speak for itself.

"Don't be ridiculous, Splane," his mother scolded. She didn't look at me or thank me, simply changed directions and went to the baker, through the front door. Splane hurried to follow her.

I hoped that would help end some of the animosity they had toward me. Walking back to the cottage, I pondered the candle maker's tale, unsure who in that story I needed to free or teach. Part of me was inclined to believe it was the Liege Lord trapped in the estate like the candle maker suggested, but why would I want to free such a bane? Perhaps that's what he needed to be taught...proper behavior.

As I neared the cottage, the goat bleated pathetically in the back, so I walked around to investigate. There, within sight of the open doors, Tennen had Bryn pinned to a mound of fresh hay. Her skirts were hiked up to her waist and her legs wrapped around Tennen's rapidly pumping, naked backside. Neither noticed me.

I pivoted back around the corner and pressed myself against the wall, out of sight and in shock. The goat's bleat drowned out most of their mingled moans. After a few moments it quieted, their moans and the goat's protests over their use of her bedding.

"Tennen," I heard Bryn say softly. "My father wants me to marry soon."

"You are of an age."

I cringed for my sister loving such a fool.

"As are you," she said.

In the silence, I heard the soft rustle of clothes being righted.

"I would be a good wife," Bryn said.

"Why would I want to marry you when I've already fucked you? It's nothing special anymore."

Hearing her soft gasp, I quickly moved to the front of the cottage and let myself in. Not trusting either of them, I hid in Father's study. How could Bryn give him so much of herself? Hadn't she seen the type of man he was? He reminded me of the Liege Lord in the candle maker's story. How many Bryns had he left behind? Poor Bryn. I wanted to go out and comfort her, but she would not react kindly to my knowing her shame. She'd given herself and been rejected for it.

So, I waited quietly in the office. When the cloud-covered sky dimmed enough to indicate Father's impending return, I slipped out the window. The dress hampered me—it was more of an inelegant tangle and fall out of the window—but I managed to leave the house without being detected. I circled the woods in front of the cottage to step out onto the path and reapproached our home from a distance.

Bryn didn't look up from whatever it was she stirred on the stove, but it didn't matter. The desolation on her face was plain to see.

"Is Blye home?" I asked, truly wondering where she'd been through Tennen's visit.

"No. She took a few of her creations to the seamstress this morning and hasn't been back." She barely whispered the words, and as soon as she finished speaking, she went out the back door without a word.

I didn't stay to listen to her soft sobs but fled once again to Father's study to read about plants.

AT DINNER, Father announced his plans to travel to Water-On-The-Bridge the next day. He had many books in his library and knew he couldn't leave them all to move in one trip, so he hired a wagon and asked if either of my sisters would like to join him. Both promptly said yes, though for very different reasons. Blye explained she wanted to speak with the seamstresses there to see if she could apprentice for room and board, a sure way to lengthen the time limit of remaining unwed so she could seek a suitable contender. Bryn stated plainly that no one in Konrall would ask for her, and she would like the chance to meet the eligible men the Water had to offer.

Father agreed to take them both and asked that I stay to teach his class. With a feeling of dread, I agreed.

THE NEXT MORNING, we worked together to load the wagon, which Splane had driven over at dawn. Bryn made no comment about Tennen's whereabouts. With the back loaded with books carefully packed in crates and covered with oiled cloth, Father eyed the dark skies.

"We'd best be off," he said to my sisters. He handed me his lesson plan for the day, hugged me farewell, and climbed aboard to take the reins. They left me standing by the cottage door, and only Father gave a backward glance.

"Watch for us near dinner," he called before they disappeared into the trees.

I walked the path to the schoolhouse, warily watching for Tennen and Splane, unsure if the blunt silver had helped our relationship or not. When Splane dropped off the wagon, he'd spent so much time gaping at Bryn, he hadn't spared me a glance. The Coalre boys couldn't keep a secret, it would seem.

The butcher's daughter, Magdaline, stood at the school doors waiting for me. Twelve and shy, she chirped a surprised greeting at me, her eyes wide.

"I'm teaching in my father's place today," I said with an amused smile. "I hope that's okay."

She nodded enthusiastically.

The day went quickly with only a handful of students in attendance. I followed my father's lesson plan and enjoyed the children's wit. It felt odd thinking of them as children when only a few years separated us.

Finally, I dismissed them and closed the schoolhouse doors. A steady rain fell outside. Walking the path in the evening light didn't bother me as much as the rain did. I jogged along the path, reaching the cottage quickly. The kitchen felt cool and damp since the stove had gone out. I relit the fire and warmed my fingers before searching for something to eat.

A slight scrape on the floor alerted me that I wasn't alone. Spinning, I watched Tennen take another step closer to me, having just come from Father's study. His dry hair and cruel leer told me enough of his intentions that I knew I needed to run. Again. The door leading to the backyard waited to my left and the door to the front of the cottage to my right.

Frozen, we eyed each other. One chance. I cursed my dress, steeled myself, and feinted to the right. Tennen bolted into action, moving toward the front door as I shifted my weight and sprinted for the back.

Behind me, I heard him slip and curse, but I didn't stop. The back door banged loudly against the outside wall as I shoved it open and flew into the rain. I hiked my skirts high to free my legs. North. Refuge. The rain-slicked ground slid easily underfoot as I tried to run. The sound of Tennen's close pursuit set my heart racing. I'd never make it. I danced around the sparse trees and ducked under the occasional branch, panting and struggling to keep my footing while hoping Tennen wouldn't.

A wall of mist stood before me, and I shouldered into it, losing myself for a moment.

The skirts grew heavier as they soaked up the falling rain, and my arms burned with their weight. I slid and fell forward, too late dropping the skirts as the ground rose to meet me. I landed hard on my stomach and my face hit the ground with enough force that it bounced. Thankfully, hitting the spongey ground didn't hurt much.

Tennen, who'd been on my heels, tripped on my skirts before I could scramble to my feet and landed heavily atop me. The impact drove the air from my lungs in a great oof. We lay like an X on the ground, his torso crossed over mine, effectively pinning me.

He laughed above me.

"You never had a chance."

I couldn't answer. I could barely breathe with his weight on me. I tried struggling, but the mud that cushioned my fall made it impossible to do anything more than flail.

"Ho, ho! What's this?" he said, touching one of my bared legs.

I struggled harder, but his hand just slid over my mud-coated skin, inching its way upward.

He put his free hand in my hair and pulled back hard, forcing me to arch off the ground. He leaned in toward my ear, never stopping his exploration. "No stockings? Naughty, Benella. Maybe I had the wrong sister."

His hot breath fanned my cheek, and my anger boiled. I arched further back, trying to hit his head with my own as I'd done before. He laughed.

"Not this time."

His fingers found the edge of my covering and slid underneath to stroke my buttocks. I screamed in fury, twisting sharply. The move pulled out some of my hair. He tried to hold me tight, but the mud and the rain made me too slippery to grip. I struggled further, clawing a handful of mud and decaying vegetation. Twisting, I slapped my handful of glop across his face, effectively blinding him. He grunted and pushed my head away, releasing my hair.

As he shifted to the side to wipe at his eyes, I took the opportunity and scrambled out from under him. Full of mud, I struggled to gain my feet and when I did, I slid more than I walked.

"You think you're any different from the rest of us?" he cried.

"No," I yelled back at him while looking for something I could use to bash him over the head. "How can I possibly be any different? Look at me." The frustration over his blind, illogical hatred pooled in my blood.

"We all look at you," he said. "You're too good to look back. And when you do, it's to look down your nose at us."

He climbed to his feet, towering over me, hate plain on his face. His statement stunned me, and I stared at him with a frown. I'd never looked down on anyone. Had I? I gave what I could to the butcher to help those less fortunate. I'd even helped Tennen's mother. How could that be looking down on anyone? I opened my mouth to protest but stopped when I felt something circle my waist. Tennen laughed as I looked down. Vines looped around me and began tugging me backward. Were they here to protect me and give me refuge? With the estate, I never knew what to expect.

My gaze flew to Tennen, and his eyes narrowed on me.

"How many times have you gone to the estate and walked away uninjured?"

"Never uninjured," I said with a snort. I didn't clarify that the injuries were due to him and his brother or self-inflicted.

The vines pulled, and I slid several inches along the ground. Another vine crept along the ground beside me, extending toward Tennen. He saw the vine and eyed me dispassionately.

"I hope you're hurt even worse this time."

Then he turned and walked away, leaving me behind.

I tried standing, but the vines didn't loosen. The one that had crept toward Tennen curved and wrapped around me instead. The single vines twisted together to create a thick rope that hefted me into the air and once again moved me toward the estate in a slow shuffle.

CHAPTER SIX

THE VINES DEPOSITED ME JUST INSIDE THE FIRMLY closed gate. Muddy rivulets ran from my clothes, and I tilted my face toward the falling rain to wash away the mud still clinging to my skin.

A voice from the gloom startled me.

"What would you have of me this time?" the beast asked.

I spotted a large, dark shape to my right and tried to focus on it through the rain as I began to shiver. The warmth I'd worked up from the run had left during the slow passage here.

"Refuge," I said, stammering with cold. "I can't return home until my father does."

The beast grunted, and the shape to my right moved, growing larger as it rose from its crouched position.

"Follow me," he said, moving into the falling darkness.

Hesitantly, I followed, wrapping my arms around myself as my wet skirts clung to my legs. His shape always remained far enough in front of me that I could never quite see him clearly. Eventually, a large structure loomed before us, its details hidden in the enchanted mist that filled the estate at its whim.

Ahead, something made a soft creak of protest. I followed the noise and found an open door leading to a vast, dark, cold room. I stepped inside, glad to be free of the rain.

"Light the fire and warm yourself," his disembodied voice said from the darkness. "Walk straight ahead. You will find what you need."

Arms extended, I shuffled forward in the dark until I touched stone. Running my fingers lightly along the porous surface, I discovered I stood before an enormous hearth. Head level, a stone mantel held what I needed to light the fire. I blew on my fingers to dry them before attempting a spark. It took several tries to start the waiting tinder; but when I did, I felt an overwhelming surge of relief. The tiny bit of light the small flame threw into the room helped dispel some of the gloom. I looked out into the wall of black surrounding me and wondered where he waited. The faint outline of the still open door was the only other object I could see outside the circle of light.

For the next several minutes, I fed the hungry flame.

Soon, it cast enough heat that I could sit back on my heels and warm my hands.

"I will check for word on your father's return. Stay here in your refuge," he growled in a curiously angry tone. The door slammed closed.

Why had he gotten angry? Looking around, I saw nothing that might suggest an answer. Standing, I moved to the woodbin set back from the fire and took some larger pieces to place on the established flames. In a few minutes, only a few black shadows remained in the furthest corners of the room, and I clearly saw my surroundings.

I stood in a large kitchen, and it appeared as if it had been ransacked. Pots lay on their sides on the floor, a table near one wall had been splintered in two, and claw marks savaged just about every surface. My stomach dipped a little at the evidence not to trust the beast's precarious kindnesses.

With the new light, I saw how caked with mud I remained. My dress was heavy with it, and it clung to my legs. The muck would itch when it dried. Walking around the kitchen, I found a hand pump for water and a large kettle with a handle. Doggedly, I worked to fill the kettle then struggled with its weight as I crossed the room and set it on the metal arm above the fire. Using a rod to nudge the arm, I swung the pot toward the back of the hearth so it dangled just above the dancing flames.

Searching again, I found a few cloths that appeared

relatively clean and a very large wooden tub. I stared at the tub for a long while, debating. He'd promised refuge, but could I trust it enough to wash? No. I left the tub where it lay upside down in a corner of the room and fetched another pot of water.

I tried washing with the first tepid pot, but my dress was too coated with mud. Every time it touched a newly cleaned spot of skin, it left a mud streak. Sighing, I dragged the tub over to the fire. I filled it a quarter of the way with cold water and then dumped in a pot of boiling water. With patience, I slowly filled the tub halfway with water, then I stood staring at it. The mud on my scalp had dried, pulling my skin tight. I wanted to be clean but didn't know when the beast would return. Eyeing the door, I went to the broken table and dragged half of it over to the tub. Standing on its short edge, it made a modest privacy screen. I could use it to dry my dress, too.

The water began to cool as I debated. I knew I shouldn't. I would regret it without a doubt. Something bad would happen. Surely only an idiot would undress in a strange house with an angry beast lurking about. But he'd promised refuge. My scalp ached where Tennen had pulled out the hair, and the mud on my legs was making me itchy. Even with the fire blazing, it didn't warm the room or dry me fast enough to drive away the chill.

The curling steam from the filled tub had me hurriedly undressing.

"Idiot," I mumbled to myself.

A sigh escaped me as I sank naked into the water. With the hearth on one side and the table on the other to reflect back the heat, I relaxed a little. The tub was easily twice the size of the one we had at the cottage. I quickly ducked under the surface to rinse my hair. When I popped back up, I eyed the slightly dingy water. Rubbing my skin, I washed as best I could.

I was about to stand when the beast spoke from the darkness.

"How many times have I spared you?"

Like a startled hare, I froze, heart hammering. Blood rushed loudly in my ears, but still I strained to listen.

"Well?" he said in a growl.

"F-four," I whispered.

"Four," he agreed. "And I offered you any one thing you would have from the estate."

Shifting to my hip, I cautiously looked around but couldn't see him in either direction open to me. I looked at the table and could envision him crouched just behind it.

"What can you offer me in payment?"

"Payment?" I said, suddenly very afraid and wishing I hadn't given the blunt silver away.

"Yes," he said, growing annoyed. "Payment. What do you have?"

"Nothing," I whispered in horror. Surely he couldn't

offer me refuge then fling me over the wall to my death because I hadn't been aware it required payment.

A clicking growl echoed in the kitchen.

"Come now. Not nothing."

My heart sank as I realized what he wanted.

"*I* am not payment."

"And why not? Did I not care for you? Heal you?"

"Yes," I said slowly.

"Stand, so I can see you."

"No," I said, sinking lower in the water.

His angry roar filled the kitchen.

"You would deny me after all I've given you?"

"You mean what you gave me freely," I said bravely. "You never asked me if I wanted to be healed. You gave that freely. I never asked you to spare me."

"But I did offer you one thing," he said.

"And forced me to accept it in order for my release. You cannot demand a price for things freely given."

Smothering silence claimed the room for several awful, long minutes. The water began to cool. I continued to watch for the beast, but he made no sound. My fingers wrinkled.

"Are you still here?" I asked as my bravery began to fade.

"Yes," he said with an angry growl.

"You offered me refuge. Please leave so I can dress."

"No," he said smugly. "I will not freely give you my absence. I will need payment to leave."

I snorted before I could stop myself.

"Payment. To leave."

"Yes. Stand so I can look at you."

"I am not a whore."

"How does rising from the water make you a whore?" He laughed.

Glaring at the table, I had no answer. It didn't make me a whore, but I would feel used and cheap. I thought of my sister and cringed. I didn't want to let anyone take advantage of me like that. The fire started to die down, the flames licking the wood receded until just a few remained to dance on top the red hot coals.

"You ask too much for too little in return," I said.

"What would you have of me?"

His willingness to bargain gave me hope.

"A dry shirt to cover me. Something to eat if you have it."

"Done," he agreed too quickly. "Now stand."

His impatience worried me.

"Not yet. I want to see the shirt you have to offer me."

He roared this time.

"Do you think me a fool? When I leave to fetch it, you will rise from the water and dress."

"Had I thought of that, I probably would have," I

admitted. I'd been too worried to think that far, but as soon as he would have left the room, I was sure I would have done just that. Given his anger, I was glad he didn't leave and give me the chance.

"I will remain in this water until you return as long as it doesn't take so long that the fire dies."

Silence greeted me again. I waited a few moments and asked, "Are you there?"

No answer. Despite my promise, I considered rising from the water and dressing.

The sudden appearance of a shirt tossed over the jagged edge of the table startled me. The white material of the fine shirt seemed out of place against the wood. I quickly reached for it, but it disappeared over the edge again.

"Stand up. Now." His angry growl sounded nearby.

I really had no choice. I could sit in the water until I rotted or his anger got the better of him and he pulled me from the water regardless of his promise of refuge, or I could stand on my own and hope for the shirt.

"I'll stand," I said quietly, gripping the sides of the tub. "And when you feel you've shamed me enough, feel free to reward me with a shirt."

I stood facing the table, hoping it would offer me a bit of modesty since it came to my waist. And it did until he flung it to the side. The dying fire and the long shadow I cast hid him again, and I hoped the lack of light hid me as well. I wanted to close my eyes but dared not. Instead, I looked down and stepped over the edge of the tub.

"Shame," he whispered. "There is no shame in this. Only desperation." He sounded slightly sad.

I didn't have time to reflect on it because the shirt sailed out of the darkness and landed on my head, blinding me. The door opened and closed before I could pull it from my face. Quickly putting my arms through the sleeves, I threaded the buttons through their holes before turning to add more wood to the fire. As I guessed, I stood in the kitchen, alone once again.

My dress lay in a heap on the floor. I thought of putting it back on, but then wondered what I'd do. Unless my father had returned, there was as little safety for me outside the estate as there was inside. Sighing, I tossed my dress into the bath water. After rinsing it as best I could, I wrung it out and hung it over the edge of the table, which I again pushed close to the fire.

It took me a while to empty the tub with the bucket, but eventually I had all the water outside, and I turned the tub upside down and used it as a chair. The long shirt fell to the tops of my knees when I stood. When I sat, it rode a bit higher in back, but protected me enough that I didn't have to sit bare bottomed.

My eyes grew heavy as I waited for the dress to dry,

and the stack of wood beside the hearth grew smaller. My stomach growled, and I recalled my request for food. Standing, I searched for something on the kitchen shelves and found a surprising bounty of hard cheese and dried fruit. I took a small portion of each and sat back by the fire.

After about an hour passed, the door flew open again. My heart pounded within its boney cage, and I moved to turn around, but his words stopped me.

"Do not turn. Stay as you are." He sounded angry. Beyond angry, actually. His growl was so severe it was hard to understand him.

I stayed still, staring at the flames while I strained to hear him move. Suddenly he spoke from right behind me as he gently touched my hair, his tone conflicting with his touch.

"Your payment went to waste."

Unsure what he meant, I remained quiet. He touched a tender spot near the crown of my head, and I flinched.

"Hurt again, girl?"

"Benella," I murmured, very uncomfortable with him standing so close behind me.

"Not a pretty name," he said with less of a growl.

"It's after my father and mother," I said slowly as his touch feathered over my head as if trying to find where I was hurt. "My mother had hoped after two daughters, the third would be a boy and planned to name him after my father, Benard. When I arrived, she'd been so upset that my father had suggested I still carry part of his name and hers as well, Nadelle. Benella is better than Nadard."

The beast gave a surprised grunt, and he parted my hair. I knew what he intended and leaned forward out of his way.

"I cannot accept any more from you without knowing the price."

He snorted.

"I give this freely." He tugged me back and touched his tongue to my head for a second time. I wondered what he'd do if he got a strand of hair in his mouth, but then supposed licking my head wasn't so different from licking his own furry hide.

It soothed the bare patches so much that I began to doze and leaned back against him. His warmth cradled me, and I fell asleep.

At some point during the night, strangely muffled sounds of cawing roused me from a deep sleep. Curled on my side, I snuggled deeper into the pile of furs lying under me. From the darkness, something growled softly and silenced the bird as a large, warm hand soothed my hair. I sank back into my slumber.

In the morning, I stretched with a yawn and groaned. The cold cobble floor made me ache, and I sat up with a shiver and a frown. Hadn't there been a pile of furs last night? Studying the kitchen, lit now by the sun that shone through several windows set high on the walls, I saw only my dress, boots, and underthings. No furs.

Recalling the hand on my head, my mouth popped open. The beast. I sprang to my feet and looked around, the shirt brushing my legs. Everything clicked back into place, and I hurried to dress as I worried what Father might be thinking.

I hesitated to take the shirt as I couldn't remember how I'd asked for it. Unsure if it really belonged to me now or not, I folded it neatly and set it on the broken table with a look of regret.

WHEN I WALKED into the cottage looking disheveled, Bryn only spared me a censuring glance; and I knew I'd arrived in an untidy state too often in recent days. She washed dishes in a small tub on a plank counter near the stove. The table was empty and only the lingering hint of cooked food perfumed the air.

"Go borrow one of Father's shirts. You'll need to wash your dress before you can wear it anywhere. Father wants us looking presentable tonight. We're to dine with the Kinlyn family." Her flat tone told me what she thought of the idea, so I didn't ask any questions about why we were going. At least I would get to eat.

Father's bedroom door stood open, the trunk for his clothes at the foot of his bed clearly visible. Feeling intrusive, I knelt before the trunk and tipped the lid back. I hadn't ever looked in Father's trunk, as I never did the laundry. Bryn washed everything, folded it, and tucked it neatly away.

Inside the trunk, two distinct piles of clothes defined my father's sad wardrobe. On the right, his two neatly folded white shirts and spare pair of trousers waited for their next use. The left pile doubled what the right had to offer with the addition of two neckcloths, worn and frayed, lying on top. Everything in the left pile had been patched or mended in some way. Loose threads dangled from frayed sleeve cuffs and patches adorned knees.

Carefully moving aside the neckcloths, I took the top shirt from the mended pile and shook it out. It would service for wearing on my treks in the woods and for around the cottage. I placed the neckcloths neatly back into the trunk and closed the lid.

In my room, I glanced once at Blye's trunk of cloth and pushed back my resentment. I knew she mended his clothes and did a good job of it too, but she could easily make Father a new shirt. Was it fair to resent her when I'd ignored my own opportunity to help Father? After all, I'd slept in a very fine shirt Father could have used. Granted, it would have been a bit large, but Blye could make a shirt smaller. She'd proven that already.

Dressed in my familiar trousers and a borrowed, threadbare shirt, I bunched up my dress and took it outside where Bryn usually did the washing in good weather. Then, I began the long process of hauling water and soaping, scrubbing, twisting, and rinsing the dress. The process had to be repeated several times until the cloth began to look blue again. Giving it a final wring, I tossed it over a line Bryn had tied outside and wiped my hands on my pants.

My stomach growled, and I eyed the sky. Inside, the cottage remained quiet, and I wondered where Blye had gone. Wrinkling my nose at the thought of going inside, I set off walking east away from the village and the estate to see what the woods might offer me to eat. Though my intentions to stay away from the estate were pure, my mind kept going back to the shirt and the cheese; and soon, my feet were taking me north.

First, I checked the ground by the tumbled rock and found peas growing so thick that the plants twined together into a solid blanket. I stopped to pick a few, nibbling them to take the edge off my hunger, then stuffed a handful into each pocket, regretting my lack of a bag.

Continuing on, I walked the perimeter of the wall until I reached the gate, which swung open in a slow, loud arc to announce my presence. Assuming nothing, I stayed standing outside of the estate and looked over my shoulder, eyeing the peaceful trees behind me. Shadows claimed those nearest the estate, but in the distance I could make out some sun dappled branches.

Swallowing hard and hoping no one stood near enough to hear, I looked back into the shadowy estate and called out, "Are you there?"

Silence answered me.

"The shirt...I left it because I wasn't sure if you meant for me to keep it or not. If you did..." Nothing inside the estate stirred. My stomach growled, and I reached into my pocket for another peapod. I chewed thoughtfully, enjoying the crisp sweetness while wondering if he waited somewhere inside, listening to me.

After several long moments, I gave up and turned back the way I'd come. I harvested more peas and carried home what I'd picked in the loose ends of my shirt.

Leaving all but a handful of my harvest on the kitchen table for Bryn to do with as she would, I secluded myself in Father's study, picking a book at random to entertain myself until dinner. Occasionally, Bryn or Blye's quiet voices would break through my concentration, but never long enough to listen to what they said.

Father arrived home and, with a twinkle in his eyes, complimented me on my new shirt. I met his smile with a grin of my own as I replaced the book I'd just finished and went to check on my dress. The damp air hadn't helped the cloth dry through, so I was forced to wear a slightly soggy dress to the Kinlyn's.

They lived close to two miles outside of town to the south, a long walk for Bryn and Blye, who never ventured further than the village on foot. Both walked side-by-side quietly matching steps as if on a march. Father and I walked behind them. Other than his cheery greeting to me when I'd returned home, he'd said little. Unlike their subdued moods, I happily looked forward to dinner. Anticipation of a good meal was only part of it. This would be my first official dinner at someone else's home.

Mrs. Kinlyn, who I'd never met directly but had seen in the village on a few occasions, stood in the doorway of their modest home, watching for us. The trees had been cleared from around the house for quite a distance to allow for an animal shed and several fields. Uprooted trees at the edge of the fields, bordering the woods beyond, foretold of bigger fields for next year's crops.

"Welcome," Mrs. Kinlyn said with a smile as she motioned for us to enter. She looked close to Father's age, perhaps a bit older, with windburned, brown skin. Tiny white lines fanned from the corners of her eyes from squinting in the sun. I found her happy smile infectious and smiled in return. My sisters murmured polite greetings.

Inside the square home, a single wall divided the room in half. At one end of the room, a long table with several chairs around it took up most of the space along with the hearth. The other side of the room held the kitchen with a modern iron oven. Two closed doors interrupted the plain wall, and I guessed they led to bedrooms.

At the table, six men sat waiting. Well, almost men since the youngest looked about nine. They all appeared freshly washed, and I bet they wore their best clothes like we did. The Kinlyn children had all inherited their mother's smile.

"Please, sit. Everything's ready. Henick, help me with the roast, please," Mrs. Kinlyn said.

One of the older boys stood to help his mother while Mr. Kinlyn rose to greet Father and shake his hand. Introductions were made. Henick, the oldest at twenty, smiled when his father said his name. Renald, the next at eighteen, nodded politely, his smile never wavering. Kennen, close to my own age, winked at me when his father said his name. I wanted to wink back, but all eyes were on me so I just smiled in return. The introductions ended with Bolen and, finally, Parlen.

Mr. Kinlyn directed us to our seats with Father and me sitting near Mr. and Mrs. Kinlyn, and Bryn and Blye sitting at the other end of the table with Henick and Renald. Seeing the arrangement, I knew I had been correct in the purpose behind the dinner. The youngest, Parlen, sat to my right with Kennen across from me.

I listened with half an ear to Henick and Renald's

attempts to converse with my sisters. They politely asked after the interests of my sisters, but neither answered in enough detail to inspire an intelligent response. So the brothers started explaining about their father's plans for their crops. I couldn't understand Bryn and Blye. All of the Kinlyn men were handsome enough and had pleasant natures. Why weren't they giving them a chance?

"What do you do here, Parlen?" I asked the sandy blonde boy sitting beside me.

He politely wiped his mouth before answering. "When we need to dig around a tree before pulling it, I help with the digging. Otherwise, it's care for the animals and hunt for game."

"Really? What do you hunt?" interest spurred me to ask.

"Mostly rabbit and wild hen," he said. "But once I came this close to bagging a wild pig." He held his thumb and forefinger up with an inch of space between.

Kennen laughed and picked up the story.

"He's lucky the pig escaped the trap before he tried to wrestle him down. It had tusks enough to bleed him."

"Kennen," Mrs. Kinlyn said in quiet warning.

The only good conversation to be heard and it wasn't fit for the dinner table. I suppressed a sigh and tried again.

"I trap rabbit, mostly. We don't have anything else wild so near the village. If I cross the river to the east, I can usually find some type of bird."

"River?" Parlen perked up.

"It runs south, just east of the village," I said slowly, trying to visualize how far it might be from the Kinlyn farm. "I'd think you'd run into it less than an hour's walk east."

"S'True," Mr. Kinlyn said in his quiet way. "Runs slow and deep for a bit."

"Good fishing?" Renald asked with interest. All of the Kinlyn boys watched their father closely.

Mr. Kinlyn laughed slowly.

"Looks like we should rest the trees tomorrow and try for some fish."

The boys agreed with a laugh. Liking the happy calm atmosphere of their home, I listened to their plans and ate until my stomach ached.

THE WALK home seemed to take longer, but at least we didn't walk in silence. Father asked Blye what she thought of Renald.

"He seems nice enough, but I'd still like to try to apprentice at a seamstress in Water-On-The-Bridge. The one we visited yesterday wanted to see an example of my work and said she would consider me if it was well done."

Father nodded without comment and then asked Bryn what she thought of Henick.

"If I marry him, I will die before my time," Bryn ominously predicted.

I wanted to ask her how she could possibly know when her *time* was but kept silent.

Father made no comment either.

CHAPTER SEVEN

THE SUN SET AS WE FOLLOWED THE MAIN ROAD TO THE village. In the distance, the baying cry of a lonely dog broke the evening's quiet. The scuff of our footfalls on the packed earth kept us company.

When we returned home, a large chest rested on the ground in front of our door. Attached to the clasp, a single piece of crisp parchment fluttered in the slight breeze. Father plucked up the paper before any of us could move close enough to read it and brought it inside, heading for his study. Bryn and Blye stared at the chest for a moment, neither moving to touch it. Skirting around it as Father had, I followed him to the study. After a brief delay, I heard Bryn and Blye follow.

"It would appear news of your need to marry has spread," he mumbled looking troubled. "This note worries me."

He handed the sheet over for us to read.

Sir,

This trunk is but an example of what I can offer for your daughter should you willingly part with her this very night.

Be warned, once you part, you will never meet again. If you consent, have her await me alone outside your front door in place of the trunk. If I find the trunk as I left it, I will know you have declined.

I COULDN'T MAKE sense of the scrawled signature that decorated the bottom of the page.

Neither Bryn nor Blye spoke as they both left to see what the trunk held. Father followed them while I narrowed my eyes on the writing. Who would mysteriously want to take one of them after the sun fell? And the request hinted that he had no desire to meet Father in person.

Setting the letter on Father's cluttered desk, I slowly followed the sound of an excited squeal.

"Look at this!" Blye cried, pulling out a long length of smooth material that rippled in a cascade when she draped it over her arm.

Leaning close, I eyed the contents of the trunk.

Obviously, the mysterious suitor meant for Blye to join him. Neither Bryn nor I had much care for material, though watching Bryn's appraising gaze, I guessed she might be gaining an appreciation for it.

"I've never felt anything so fine," Blye whispered, gently stroking the fabric. "To wear this...I would feel like a princess."

"So you'd accept some unknown man?" Bryn asked.

"Wouldn't you for this kind of wealth?" Blye said with a laugh.

Neither looked at Father, but I watched them all as they spoke. Father studied the contents warily. Blye saw nothing more than the wealth, not even the jealousy in Bryn's gaze.

"I cannot allow it," Father said finally.

Blye's head whipped toward him; her disbelief plain. He held up a hand before she could protest.

"The wealth is alluring, but what if the man or your place in his life is not. I recall Bryn's words about the Kinlyn's hard life. They are a happy family with wealth enough of their own, but Bryn knew it wasn't enough. You know nothing about him, and I fear sending you off into an unknown life without the assurance that I might check on you occasionally."

Blye said nothing as tears spilled over from her eyes and slowly rolled down her cheeks.

"We will not reject the offer outright, however," he

said. "I will write a reply to leave with the trunk explaining a father's need for assurances of wellbeing and happiness."

Blye nodded and began folding the material with Bryn's help as Father turned to retreat into his study once more. Blye could cry her pretty tears, but she was foolish to think wealth enough of a basis to marry a man. Look at the baker. He had plenty of wealth, but would that be enough to lie still each night as he lay beside me? I shivered at the thought. No amount of wealth would make that image pleasant enough to endure.

Leaving them to their cloth, I crept to our room to change from my dress. Having worn it as it finished drying, my skin felt itchy; and I couldn't wait to put on my loose nightgown and scratch my stomach.

In the dim light of the room, something white stood out on my coverlet. Lighting the single candle stub we reserved for emergencies, I found the shirt I'd worn the night before laid out neatly on my bed. My stomach dipped. The beast had heard me at the gate. But why hadn't he answered then? Why bring it to the cottage?

Hearing someone approach, I quickly blew out the candle and plucked the shirt from the bed. Blye shuffled into the room and mumbled that she was tired. I left the room, hiding the shirt from her view and knocked on Father's study.

He called for me to enter in a slightly harassed tone. Feeling guilty for interrupting him, but not wanting either of my sisters to see the shirt before he did, I opened the door and slipped inside.

"I'm sorry for interrupting, but I wanted to give this to you." I held out the shirt.

When he looked up from his writing and his eyes focused on what I held, he set his ink aside. "Not from the chest, but just as fine," he deduced. "Where did it come from?"

"The estate," I said without reservation. I'd gathered so many odd things from the enchanted estate it rarely drew any notice when I came home with something new. Though, everything in the past had been something to eat.

"This is a surprise. Tell me how you came by it exactly," he said, standing and taking it from me. He studied it closely, missing my blush.

I couldn't retell all of the details, just enough to appease his curiosity.

"Tennen was in the cottage when I returned from the school. There was no doubting his intentions. I ran out the back door straight toward the estate, hoping to lose him in the mist." I decided to skip the part where Tennen had almost caught me, too. "The estate let me enter, giving me refuge and that shirt because I was soaked from the rain."

He listened intently and looked up from the shirt when I finished.

"The rain kept us on the road longer than I'd planned," he said. "I had anticipated returning before you returned from the schoolhouse. When we didn't, I worried about you. Then, arriving home late and finding your bed empty..." He sighed. "I'm very relieved you weren't forced into..." He shook his head unable to finish.

"Staying at the estate wasn't so bad," I admitted.

"I advise you to avoid going near it for a while. The beast neither forgets nor forgives trespassers. You're very fortunate to have walked away as many times as you have."

Watching him walk to his chair behind the desk, I realized he wasn't referring to my jaunts to search for food, but that he knew about my other trespasses. I didn't wonder how. As the schoolteacher, he heard all the whispered rumors from the village children. No doubt someone had witnessed or heard something.

"At the time of each trespass, I feel I made the best choice of those given me."

"You usually do," he said with a half-smile. "Now excuse me while I compose a hopefully polite refusal to an unknown person. Tomorrow, I'll ask the baker if he noted anyone of interest passing through."

My stomach sank, but not with mention of the baker. The arrival of the shirt on my bed and the trunk at the door could not be coincidence.

"Father, it bothers me that this suitor mentioned no name, just wrote daughter. Perhaps when you word your reply, you could mention Blye's name so there is no mistake about which daughter this person would expect if you come to an agreement."

Father made a thoughtful noise and nodded. Already his eyes drifted to the window as he sank into thought. I left him quietly with his new shirt and crept to my own bed.

I woke late after having trouble sleeping the night before. The sun already rose above the treetops when I stepped outside dressed in trousers and Father's old shirt. I finished braiding back my hair as I walked east toward the river. My bag bounced gently against my hip with nothing but a bit of string and a hook in it. Today, I'd fish.

At the stream, I peeled off my boots and socks. The chill from the spring ground penetrated my feet, but I ignored it as I rolled up my pant legs. I'd fished before and knew the risks. Hooks were precious, and if the line pulled too taut, I would be forced to step into the water. Walking home with cold wet feet would make for a miserable journey.

Finding a long, straight branch thin enough to hold over the water proved to be a bit of a challenge. It took me a good hour, and I wished I hadn't been so careless with my old rod last summer. I'd accidentally stepped on it while pitching hay into the shed for the goat. Since I typically stored it in the rafters, I had no idea why it'd been on the ground in the first place. I'd been especially careful with it because I'd had such luck—we had fish for almost three weeks straight—before the fatal break.

After peeling offshoots from the branch, I tied the string on the end, baited my hook, and set to work enjoying a quiet afternoon while nibbling on day-old peapods. Too soon, I had enough fish to fill my string. While sitting on the bank to put on my socks, a loud caw from across the stream slowed my progress as I looked up. Perched on a thick branch of a tree on the other side of the stream, a crow watched me with one eye while its head turned toward the north.

"Mr. Crow, are you following me?" I asked with amusement. It blinked an eye at me but remained quiet.

As long as it only watched, I didn't mind its presence. I didn't, however, want it driving me back to the estate. After tugging on the last boot and tying the lacing, I pulled the smallest fish from my line and set it on the ground.

"Here you go."

I stood and casually walked away. When I heard a rapid flap of wings, I casually looked over my shoulder and watched the crow land and feast on the fish. Smiling, I journeyed home, lengthening my strides so the fish didn't turn bad before I got there.

Bryn didn't look too pleased when I presented her with a dozen fillets.

"I hope I marry soon," she muttered. "I won't tolerate another three weeks of fish."

Realization about what had actually happened to my old fishing pole hit me, and I took care to hide the current pole well before returning to clean up the fish remains. It was smelly business, but the garden did well when I buried the remains.

Washing up outside with a harsh lye soap to rid myself of the smell, I wasn't surprised to hear the flap of wings and a caw nearby. The crow sat perched on the shed roof.

"Sorry," I said, watching the creature while I dried my hands. "I buried the remains of the others in the garden."

"I need you to buy some flour," Bryn called from inside.

I made a face. I had avoided the baker since he'd stopped by to speak with Father. Why would I march right into his store?

"Please ask Blye."

"I can't go!" Blye cried from the open window of our bedroom. "I'm working on the dress to show the seamstress in the Water, and Father's asked me to take in a shirt he somehow acquired."

It pleased me to know he didn't tell Blye the shirt came from me or, rather, the estate through me. She would insist I go back and try to procure more clothes. But I didn't like that she refused to fetch the flour.

"Bryn, can't you go?"

"I'd rather not face..."

I sighed. Her need to avoid Tennen was due to wounded pride over her own stupidity. My reason to avoid the baker was self-preservation. Still, I knew I'd go.

"Fine. I'll need to change." I wouldn't walk into the village wearing a threadbare shirt that easily displayed the outline of my bindings.

"Just hurry," Bryn said impatiently. Holding in the urge to make a face at her, I marched to our room, where Blye sat on the bed concentrating on her stitching, and quickly changed into the dress.

When I went to the kitchen to ask Bryn for the coin I needed for the flour, she handed me peas. I wanted to scream. Instead, I stomped my way into the village, marched through the front door of the bakery and asked to speak with Mrs. Medunge. Of course, the baker's sister went to fetch him instead.

"Benella," he said when he walked through the door from the back. "So lovely today. What can I do for you?"

"I'd like to trade these peas for flour," I spoke woodenly, setting the cloth wrapped bundle on the counter. It was the same cloth they'd loaned for the flour the first time.

"I'm sorry, my dear—"

I would never be his dear.

"—but I can't trade. It's coin only. If others heard I

accepted produce for flour, no one would want to pay me coin again, and I'd be overrun with produce."

"I understand." I scooped up the peas with two hands and left the cloth on the counter. "The cloth is yours. Good day." I turned to leave.

"Wait. I hate seeing you leave upset. Come in back, and we'll talk."

I kept walking, and he called after me again. Next, I went to the butcher and asked if he would trade a copper for the peas. He apologized and explained that he'd taken trade in payment for the last several days and had no coin, affirmation that the baker's assessment of trade had a grain of truth. When I stepped out, the baker stood in the door and silently waved me back across the street; but I had another option left to me. Cutting diagonally across the road, I used the toe of my boot to knock at the candle maker's door.

The candle maker opened the door for me after several long minutes, during which I endured the baker's constant stare.

"Benella, come in," he said with a small smile. "What do you have there?"

"Peapods. Would you be willing to trade? I need a copper to buy flour."

"Ah." He nodded in understanding, holding out his hands. My shoulders sagged in relief.

"What happened to the blunt silver?"

Groaning before I stopped myself, I admitted, "I gave it to someone who needed it more."

"Interesting that Mrs. Coalre came in just yesterday to buy a candle. I thought they were out of coin, too."

I remained quiet and watched him set the peas on his table so he could shuffle over to a shelf.

"I'm not one for peas, but you allowed me to hold the flowers without asking for payment, so I can hardly deny you such a small request." He plucked a coin from a very tiny pile and brought it to me.

"Thank you," I whispered, grateful for his kindness.

"Go buy your flour, dear," he said with a small wave as he settled back at his chair.

I promised myself that I would venture to the estate soon and circle it as many times as needed until it surrendered some more of those rare blooms.

The baker brightened when he saw me step from the candle maker's but frowned at my empty hands. I marched up to him, pulled a cloth from my bag—one of Father's old neckcloths—and handed him the coin without trying to step inside.

"However much flour that will buy me, please," I spoke softly, trying to keep the anger from my tone.

He turned and handed both to his sister.

"A handful, no more," he cautioned her before turning back to me with a slight scowl.

We stood several feet apart, but I felt like I faced him

toe to toe. I kept my face impassive until he heaved a sigh and let his eyes drift to my chest. Thankfully, his sister didn't leave him much time to stare.

Accepting the bag, I quickly retreated, meeting up with Father as he left the school.

"What have you been up to?" he asked, eyeing the street behind me.

"Bryn sent me for flour." I'd kept my tone pleasant, but he paused to study me.

"Very unkind," he said before walking again.

"It wasn't intentionally so," I said, defending her. "She's upset that Tennen hasn't tried to offer for her even though she knows you wouldn't agree to the match. She thought he had affection for her and isn't seeing anything beyond her wounded pride."

He said nothing. When we arrived home, I handed the flour to a mildly surprised Bryn and went to change back into my trousers. To occupy myself, I weeded the small garden while dinner cooked. In the quiet, I remembered the crow and looked to the roof of the shed.

The crow was gone.

I BELIEVED the breaded fish tasted delightful but kept that thought to myself, fearing for my new pole. Everyone ate in silence, and I wondered why. They didn't leave me wondering long.

"Do you think we'll hear anything tonight?" Blye asked.

Father set his fork aside and steepled his fingers. "I wouldn't presume to guess. The note was notoriously brief, and we have no idea if the man in question lingered in the area. Travel may have been the reason for his request to take you with him last night. We can only wait and see."

She went back to eating in silence, but the conversation had me straining to hear outside the cottage. Would we walk out in the morning to find another note on the door?

THE NEXT MORNING, nothing waited outside. Bryn started packing in earnest while Blye went back to her quiet sewing. Father, having no students to teach that day, insisted on walking with me as I foraged. Typically on the days he didn't need to teach, he used the time in his study to research. Having moved many of his books already, no doubt his reduced selection had something to do with his wish to accompany me.

The sun shone brightly as we walked toward the estate.

"Nothing from the mysterious suitor last night?" I asked, already knowing the answer.

"To your sisters' disappointment, no." He kept pace with me, watching the trees around us. Soon we came to the part where the mist crept along the bases of the trees.

"Peculiar," he said, looking up.

"What is?" I looked up but only saw the same wild, tangled vegetation I always did.

"The vines in the trees appear to be moving," he murmured, tilting his head to watch. "I heard the ones near the wall move as if alive, but this far from it? I wonder..."

I knew they moved, but said nothing, not wanting to explain how I knew. The night that Tennen had almost caught me still filled my dreams with running through the darkness.

"The place I usually visit is just ahead. The last time it offered peapods in such abundance I almost cried for not having my bag with me."

"Odd of you to leave without it," he said, focusing on me again.

Inwardly cursing my slip, I smiled sheepishly and shrugged. The mists thickened the further we went toward the estate until we only saw the immediate area around us. I wondered at the unusually menacing feel of it.

"Perhaps we should head back," I whispered, stopping abruptly to study the mist around us.

"I'm glad you think so," he returned just as softly. "I

kept quiet, trusting your expert guidance, but the feel of this place—"

I spun toward him and saw vines wrapping around his waist. His eyes were wide with shock.

"Father!" I flew toward him, tugging at the vines, but they didn't budge. More crept toward him, starting a slow familiar shuffle I knew would pull him into the estate. He read the fear on my face and tried to reassure me.

"Stay here, Benella. I'll return soon. This is only my first offense."

I kept pace with him, but the vines tugged him up into the treetops and out of my sight.

"Don't follow me," he called in warning. "You've trespassed too many times already."

Ignoring his warning, I spun and ran blindly toward the gate. Panting, I arrived to hear it creak open, barely able to make out the mist shrouded bars before me.

"Please," I begged. "My father didn't mean to trespass; he was only following me."

A growl started in the dark mist to my right, and I knew the beast waited for me.

"You refused me?"

Concerned about my father, I frowned in confusion before I realized what he meant. The trunk. I played as if I didn't understand. If the beast continued talking to me, he wouldn't be able to toss my father over the wall.

"If I recall, I did not refuse your last request of me. I

still have the shirt to prove it," I answered, still slightly out of breath.

"The trunk," he said.

"The trunk someone left for my sister, Blye? What of it?"

"The offer was meant for you," he said in a deceptively soft growl that unnerved me.

His direct answer surprised me.

"Me? Why would I need all that cloth? I don't sew. Blye does."

"You wanted a shirt. I offered the means to own several shirts."

I didn't know what to say except, "Why? Why did you offer for me?"

"You need not concern yourself with that," he growled his frustration. "Will you assent?"

"I cannot."

Birds in nearby trees screamed in protest at his rage filled roar and took flight in a rush of a dozen flapping wings.

"Only a few days ago you lay on the ground, telling me you cared not whether you lived or died. Holding so little value to your life, why not agree to my offer?"

With effort, I kept my voice soft and even to hide my fear.

"Value is an odd thing, subject to whim. What one might find value in, another might not; what has value today might not have value tomorrow, depending on the wants and needs of the evaluating individual. You prove this yourself with the same example you just provided. Several days ago when I lay on the ground indifferent to what fate might decide, you were not so interested in me. The issue is that neither of us understands the reason why we changed our minds."

He remained silent, perhaps thinking I had more to say on the matter. I didn't want to push him any further though, so I let what I said linger in the quiet for a while before speaking again.

"My father?"

"Is unharmed," he spoke softly just behind me. My stomach twitched in surprise, but I managed to quell any other reaction to his unexpected nearness.

"May I have him back, please?"

Gently, he touched the back of my head, a single stroke of my hair from crown to the tip of my braid, which ended mid-back. He lifted the braid and tugged on it slightly. I held still before him, listening to my great gusting breaths as I remembered the last time he'd touched me when I'd thought him a pile of furs.

"I will return him to you whole and healthy in hopes that you may yet change your answer, Benella," he said as his fingers threaded through my hair, loosening the braid.

As soon as my hair fell free, he disappeared.

After a few moments, I heard the rustling of leaves

above, and the mists lifted enough that I spotted Father
trussed up in the vines high above. As soon as he spotted
me, he went from looking intrigued to looking worried.

"Go, child!" he called in an urgent hush. The vines
began their stretching descent to bring him to the ground.
"I just heard the beast's roar and know he must be near
waiting for me. You shouldn't have come inside the wall."

I remained despite his urging to flee. When his feet
touched the ground, the vines loosened and then shrank
away.

"What an amazing journey," he said, watching them
for a moment before remembering where we were and the
imminent threat of the beast.

"This way," I motioned him to follow before he could
say anything. We walked through the gate, which slammed
closed behind us with a metallic clang.

For the next several days, I stayed away from the
estate, not out of fear, but because Father forbade me to
return. I struggled to find anything in the area outside of
the estate's boundaries. Though the fish were plentiful, I
knew Bryn and Blye grew tired of them. Bryn tried
cajoling me into another trip to the baker; but with nothing
to trade and her unwillingness to part with a coin, I left her
angry while I went to fish.

During this time, we entertained several more suitors, which both of my sisters rejected out of hand. Father nodded each time, accepting their answer; but I read the concern etched in his expression. Then one day, with solemn acceptance, he said we should begin packing our belongings to leave the next morning. None of us questioned him, but we all wondered how we would live in the tiny two-room house.

In the morning, Father walked to the smith to borrow the wagon he'd used last time. Into it, we packed the rest of the books, Father's bed and my sisters' bed, our trunks, cookware, and the last of our food. The desk, table, and remaining bed stayed with the house to entice the next schoolmaster. While we worked, a crow cawed at us incessantly.

When we had everything loaded, Bryn and Blye climbed onto the bench seat with Father while I sat on the backend of the wagon. The crow quieted as Father clucked the team forward, and I wondered what he would tell the beast.

We pulled onto the main road of town, and I noticed the butcher outside his door and gave a wave of farewell. The baker watched from the shadows of his porch, but I pretended not to notice. Sara stood near the quiet anvil at the smithy, looking down at the ground. I wondered what would become of her husband's dealings with the baker, knowing the blunt silver had already run out for her.

Clearing the village, the wagon jostled ponderously north until the road curved near the estate. There the woods remained eerily dark and quiet until it too passed from sight. Riding in a wagon, even if it was a butt-bruising ride, ensured a more pleasant second trip to Water-On-The-Bridge.

Arriving well before lunch, Father took a circumspect route to our new home, avoiding the main thoroughfare with its questionable businesses. We worked together to unload our belongings, cramming them into the main room of the very small house. Then Father drove the wagon back to the smith. While he was gone, Blye packed her precious dress and walked to the dressmaker, who agreed to hire her but could not offer her lodging.

Bryn and I put together Father's bed in the main room and set up their bed in the single, private room. With effort, we also managed to wedge in the three trunks. When we finished, I eyed our house with dismay.

The kitchen came equipped with a stove and dry sink like our prior cottage. Near the stove sat a table for two with two chairs. Not three feet from that, Father's bed sat against the back wall between the door to the backyard and the door to our room. A fireplace, cleverly set on an interior wall, worked to heat the main room and the room beyond.

Before the fire, a worn stuffed chair would welcome a weary scholar. To the right of the fireplace, just before a window set into the front of the house, sat a desk and several shelves that already brimmed with Father's books. To the right of that was the front door, bringing my slow turning tour to an end.

In all honesty, this house was meant for a single man or a married couple. Father had no room for any of us.

Excusing myself, I went for a walk to check the market district. Better to learn costs and who would be willing to trade right away. By dusk, I'd determined the only thing we'd changed was the size of our house. But, at least, I didn't have to worry about the baker or the smith's sons.

Sighing, I returned to our new home empty-handed. Father already pored over his books, and a very watery version of stew waited for me.

WE CELEBRATED Father's first week of pay by purchasing meat and flour. After not eating anything the prior day, all of us looked forward to the meat pie Bryn fixed. As I bit into my portion of the meat pie and gravy dripped down my chin, I thought nothing could have tasted better. However, too soon those supplies ran out, and we were back to going hungry. I noticed Father's neckcloth seemed a bit longer and the shirt that Blye had just tailored for him a little looser. My own dress gaped a bit from my waist now.

What really bothered me was Blye's success at the dress shop. She would come home talking excitedly about her customers, but never about her pay. After two weeks of living in the Water, she came home with a new dress, saying she needed to look the part to work at such an upscale shop. She gave her old dress to Bryn, who accepted it with a smile of thanks and a comment that a second dress would be handy.

That day, I put on my bag and left the village to forage. The nearby country had been picked fairly clean, so I headed in the direction I knew. Not far after passing over the bridge, I stopped until a curious wave of dizziness passed.

I trudged east, watching for signs of the estate. As soon as I saw the mist creeping around the bases of trees, I sighed with relief and turned north into the mists. The skirt of my dress still wasn't ideal for setting traps, but it was the only thing I owned that I could wear in the Water. Father's old shirt would give too many people lewd ideas.

Too soon, I reached the wall and turned to follow it east—ignoring the gate that swung open in invitation. Finally, I reached the patch of ground that usually held some sort of bounty. The sight of withered brown tops of potato plants greeted me. Using my hands, I clawed at the ground until my bag brimmed with the brown globes.

When I stood, the weight made me cringe. Carrying ten extra pounds from here to Konrall wouldn't have been a problem, but to the Water? It would be a trying journey. Still, I hoped for something in my traps as well.

Retracing my steps, I approached the gate and nearly screamed when I was pulled from behind into the maw of darkness. Two strong hands gripped my upper arms and held me against a very large, furry frame.

I didn't turn to look. I knew who had me, but I still remained unsure of his mood.

"Will you assent and stay, Benella?" he said softly.

CHAPTER EIGHT

"I cannot—"

"Then why have you returned?" he roared, hurting my ears and thrusting me away with enough force that I stumbled and lost a few precious potatoes.

"Because I'm hungry!" Angry, I picked one up, spun, and threw it into the dark. The muffled thud of the potato finding a target in the dense dark fog had me quickly regretting my loss of temper.

"I'm sorry," I whispered.

"If you had stayed, you would not be hungry."

Such an open, foolish statement. Perhaps I wouldn't be hungry because I would be dead. I kept my thoughts to myself and waited.

"So you walked from the Water just for food?"

He sounded very calm, and it worried me.

"Yes," I said.

"From my estate?"

I nodded, my throat suddenly tight.

"Then I think it fair to ask for something in return."

I remembered his last price and started to lower the bag of potatoes to the ground. I would not do that again. I wasn't in a desperate enough situation.

"Wait. Before you give up your prize and have to return home with nothing but dirt-caked nails, listen."

I paused with the bag almost touching the soil.

"I will generously give you as much food as you can carry in return for an hour of your time."

Shaking my head, I set the bag down and barely saw the potatoes spill out.

"Stubborn," he yelled in an almost inarticulate roar. "Why not?"

"I've told you once; I'm not a whore."

He growled long and loud, the sound moving around me as he circled. I wished I could see through the mist.

"Who said anything about whoring?" he said finally. "I need someone to clean the estate."

I couldn't hide my surprise.

"Just clean?"

"Yes," he ground out.

"Then, I can accept," I said, quickly bending to pick up the potatoes. Before the last one fell into the bag, he bade me to follow.

Only the sound of his footfalls led me because as we

walked, the heavy mist seemed to trail us, or at least me. It was disorienting to walk blindly ahead. Well, not blindly, but seeing less than two feet before me was hardly reassuring at the fast pace he assumed. We walked a far distance when, suddenly, the same door from my prior visit loomed ahead.

I opened the door and went inside. For a moment, I saw little; then light streamed into the room from the high windows. For a moment, I wondered about the mist that had accompanied me then apparently vanished. But, the state of the kitchen distracted me. It was just as I'd left it, the large tub upside down near the cold hearth and the table turned on its end as a privacy screen.

"What would you have me clean?" I asked. Silence answered me.

Shaking my head, I set to work righting as much of the enormous kitchen as I could. I set shelves back onto their mountings, then lined them with the various cooking pots and stirring spoons that littered the floor. I pried apart one of the table halves and set the wood near the hearth for burning. Several chairs, broken beyond repair, joined the growing pile. The remaining chairs, which had a hope of being repaired, I sat near one wall. Nothing but dust and debris carried in by the seasons remained on the floor when I finished.

Though I knew I'd spent longer than the bargained hour cleaning, I went outside in search of grass and twigs to make a rough broom. When I finished, I spent a good while longer sweeping. Satisfied with my work, I swept the last bit outside the door and went to the counter to shoulder my prize, the bag of potatoes.

When I turned back to the open door, I saw the dark mists swirling toward it and knew the beast approached. It snuffed out the sun shining through the windows and cast the room into premature evening gloom. My eyes didn't adjust quickly enough to see him move into the room, but my ears picked up his feet brushing against the cobbled floor as he strode toward me.

"You've met your end of the bargain and more. Will you return tomorrow?"

"I won't abuse your generosity," I declined carefully. "I have enough to feed us for a week if we're careful."

"A week?" He scoffed. "Come back tomorrow, and I will have sun-ripened tomatoes for you."

My mouth watered.

"And the price?"

"The same. An hour of cleaning."

I frowned as I considered the offer. He'd left me alone to clean this time, but would he do so the next time? And why did he suddenly want someone to clean for him? Food and answers were only likely if I returned.

"I'll see you tomorrow," I said.

He grunted and made another slight noise so soft and so brief I couldn't be sure what is was or what it meant.

He led me to the gate, then disappeared. The walk home wasn't as terrible as I'd anticipated. I had a rabbit to carry in addition to the potatoes, but it was the promise of tomatoes the next day that lightened my step. Before returning to the house, I traded half the potatoes for coin, hoping I wasn't making a mistake, and purchased some oats and milk for breakfast. Living in the Water, we hadn't had room for the goat; and Bryn had sold her to the butcher. I wondered where that coin had gone.

When I walked through the door with potatoes, milk, oats, and rabbit I was surprised that Bryn wasn't inside. I placed the items in the kitchen storage and went to clean up before anyone returned. Dirt smudged my dress from cleaning, so I changed into my trousers and shirt to take the dress outside and air it, which meant hanging it on the line of rope strung between trees and beating the dirt from it. After I finished, I hauled water from our private well to wash my hands and face.

By the time Bryn returned, I once again wore my dress and was reading a book while sitting comfortably in the stuffed chair before the cold hearth. She asked where I'd obtained the food, and I asked where she'd been. She didn't answer so neither did I. She lit the stove, and I listened to her start preparations for dinner. I tried not to let my mouth water.

Father said nothing when we sat down to a dinner of rabbit and baked potatoes, though he did glance at me. Just as Blye and now Bryn had their secrets, so did he. None of us knew where he taught; and when asked, he evaded the question.

THE NEXT MORNING, after a hearty meal of milk soaked hot oats, I set out for the estate better prepared.

As I had the day before, I set traps at the edge of the mist before turning north toward the gate. The dense fog of the day before didn't reappear as the gate swung open with a high-pitched screech. Instead of ignoring the invitation to enter and continuing to the dirt patch, I stepped through the gate. I wanted to leave the tomatoes on the vine until the last minute.

Within the beast's domain, only the barest hint of white mist clung to the air.

Walking north, where I thought the house should be, I gasped when an immense structure came into view. I counted two stories of windows on the wing with the kitchen and four on the main building, which extended far into the surrounding trees. I could easily clean one hour each day for the next year.

Inside, I viewed my work from the day before with satisfaction. On the butcher's block in the middle of the kitchen a note lay waiting next to a plate with cheese, bread, and a cup of cold spring water.

Eat and rest before you continue your work on the kitchen.

I set my bag beside the plate and drank deeply. Then I looked around the kitchen, wondering what else he would have me clean, until I spotted the four doors in the kitchen which had been locked the day before. All now stood ajar. The first led to a long room lined with three beds. Dust coated everything. The next door led to a hall. Walking the hall, I came to a set of steps set in the left wall. They led down into pitch black, and a cold draft drifted up to swirl around my ankles. I kept walking and found a door to the right that led to a linen closet. Everything in that room looked white and new, except again, for a fine dusting. The door at the end of the hall remained locked though I saw no keyhole.

Turning back, I retraced my steps to the kitchen. There, I took my bag to the servant's quarters and quickly changed before exploring the other doors off of the kitchen. One long room held a variety of foods, all looking surprisingly fresh. The next led to a small study filled with shelves of books. Curious, I plucked a book from its perch and opened it to find a page detailing how to dress and stuff a quail. Books on how to cook. What a splendid idea. Reluctantly, I replaced the book and returned to the main kitchen.

Though, I'd done a fair job, the hearth still needed attention. Squaring my shoulders, I set to work.

An hour later, I had removed the ash and brushed the stone clean. It hadn't been as dirty as I'd thought. I set new kindling down, ready to light should anyone have a need, and picked up the final bucket of ash. Outside, as I dumped it a few steps from the door in the overgrown weeds, I noted a swirling mass of dark fog rolling my way.

I hurried back inside and moved to the water I'd pumped after emptying the first bucket of ash. The wind had taken the dark powder and dusted me generously. By letting the water sit for an hour, I could use it without shivering. I quickly washed my hands and face. The door opened when I had a towel pressed to my face for drying.

When I opened my eyes, I could only see faint outlines of the objects in the now familiar kitchen. The shadow of the beast paced on four legs just inside the door. His back easily stood as high as my shoulders. I could make out little else about him. Yet, what little I saw was enough to make my knees weak. I rather liked the mist.

"You made better progress yesterday," he said with a low rumble.

I frowned at him.

"The work yesterday was easier." He grunted in response. "I'll just go pick my tomatoes and be on my way."

"Will you stay, Benella?" he asked quietly, confusing me.

Hadn't he just complained about my work? I was reluctant to keep giving him the same answer he'd received so poorly in the past yet had no reason to answer differently.

"I cannot," I said.

He whirled about and left with a roar. Gradually, sun began to filter back into the room. Near the door lay just enough tomatoes to fill my bag. I rushed to change and used my dirty clothes to cushion between the layers of the soft red orbs.

When I reached the gate, the beast's mist surrounded me again, forcing me to stop walking.

"Tomorrow, there will be meat if you return. As much as you can carry home in return for an hour of cleaning."

I knew I would sell the majority of the tomatoes since they didn't last long. The coin could buy meat, or it could be used to buy more milk and oats. I nodded in agreement, and the mists lifted enough that I set off for home.

As I had the day before, I arrived before anyone else. When Bryn returned she exclaimed over the tomatoes but didn't question how I'd obtained them; and I, in return, didn't ask her where she'd been.

SINCE MOVING, I slept in Father's bed and he in his chair, as there was no room for me in with my sisters. He made very little noise when he rose and hadn't yet woken me. However, exhausted from my day's work, I'd fallen asleep early. Even the slightest noise would have woken me the following morning.

Laying in the dark, I listened to him dress then walk out the back door. When I heard the scrape of the bucket as he lowered it for water, I quickly rose from bed, dressed, then once again crawled under the covers. I wanted to respect Father's unspoken wish to keep where he taught private, yet his secrecy worried me. Bryn and Blye's secrecy I could accept. It was part of who they were. But, Father had never kept secrets before.

He quietly reentered the cottage but didn't eat. He only washed and grabbed his materials for the day before leaving via the front door.

Flipping back the covers, I quickly eased the front door open and set to following him.

He headed toward the center of town, passed the Head's house, then slowed before the house of the Whispering Sisters. There, he went to the back door and nodded to the guard standing there. The guard started to nod in return, but then caught sight of me. Father turned and saw me standing half hidden behind a tree.

Even from this great distance, I saw his shoulders slump. I stepped out from my hiding place but remained near the tree as he turned to walk toward me. My heart went out to him. He was a moral man and didn't understand how a woman could go into such a trade. We'd talked about it at length on several occasions during a family dinner. I knew the lectures were to help us, his daughters, stay innocent for our future husbands.

That he'd taken a position in the house of the Whispering Sisters to educate the women there must bother him a great deal. And I knew why he'd done it. To remove me from Konrall. To keep me safe.

When he stood before me, his guilty eyes met mine.

"Benella, I—"

"Didn't eat breakfast. You can't keep doing that. I see the weight you are losing. Without you, I have no one, Father." His eyes widened in surprise. "Do they offer you food?"

He slowly shook his head, and I knew I'd puzzled him by not asking why he went there.

"Then tell the man at the door I'll be back with food for you." He opened his mouth to protest. "I won't go in. I'll just hand it to him. Eat it all."

Before he could object, I spun away toward the market district. There, I bought three pastries with the coin I had left from the prior day. I ate one pastry myself and handed two to the very stoic looking guard at the back door.

"The second one's for you if you'll ensure my father eats his portion," I said.

The man's lips twitched slightly, and I hoped that meant he agreed. I thanked him then went on my way.

The walk through the market street was peaceful so early in the morning with only the scents of baking bread to keep me company. The mill lay silent as I passed it and started my trek over the bridge.

When I reached the edge of the estate, I checked the traps I'd left overnight and was disheartened to see they remained empty. The bait I'd placed was gone. I took them down and headed into the estate.

Instead of a note, a large stag waited on the butcher block, along with an empty barrel and a burlap bag of salt. I frowned at it all. I'd watched Bryn put up salted meat when I was younger but had no idea about the particulars.

Going to the office, I paged through the books for over an hour before I found one talking about salted pork. Shrugging, I used that as a guide to butcher as best I could. I was used to skinning and cleaning small animals. A larger one proved more time consuming and messy. Blood dotted my clothes and smeared my forearms. Before I was halfway through, I lit the fire to start water heating. I would need to wash out my shirt.

Soon the barrel was full of meat, salt, and brine. I tapped the lid in place and strained to move it to the food pantry. There I found waxed cloth which I used to package the remaining meat I meant to carry home. The large carcass glistening on the butcher's block daunted me. I had no idea what to do with it. I couldn't just dump it outside the door as I had with the ash and debris.

"Sir," I called politely, thinking the title better than beast. "What am I to do with the remains?"

A dark mist swirled into the kitchen almost immediately, and I listened to the scrape of his feet on the floor. I wondered if he'd been so close all along. A few rustles of movement and then silence. The mist only lasted a moment and when it cleared, the carcass was gone, leaving only the bloodstained block.

I scrubbed the surface with a brush I found then rinsed the top thoroughly. My arms grew tired from all of the water I needed to pump. Finally, I moved to the heated water and poured it into the large tub along with some cold water. Having been foolish once, I wasn't about to bathe again. Instead, I stripped from my shirt, knowing my bindings hid the important bits, and washed my arms and face. My shirt went into the dirty water. As I was rinsing it, the mists returned. I wasn't surprised.

"Tell me you'll stay," the beast said softly. I could feel his eyes on me as I rose and set my shirt over the back of a chair near the fire.

"Tell me why you want me to," I said, bending to scoop the used water from the tub with a smaller bucket. He remained silent as I moved from the tub to the door several times. I rinsed the tub and turned it over to sit on. He moved up behind me and touched my hair.

"Will you return tomorrow?" he asked instead of answering my question.

"I don't know," I answered honestly, thinking of my father. I needed to speak with him about why he went to the Whispering Sisters. I felt certain it was in a teaching capacity, but why hide it?

The beast growled behind me.

"The next day, then."

I nodded, knowing we needed the food, and I would not be able to stay away for long.

WHEN FATHER LEFT the next morning, I didn't pretend to sleep. Instead, I rose with him. There were no oats left. I'd only been able to purchase a small amount, and Bryn had salted the meat to put in storage for hard times. I wondered how much harder our time needed to be before we could eat the meat but didn't protest her decision. However, the storage left Father and me with nothing to eat. He didn't say anything, and neither did I.

We left together, and I walked with him all the way to the Whispering Sisters then told him I would return with a pastry. He nodded and went inside.

Using my last copper, I bought him the pastry fresh from the nearest baker's oven. The glaze ran on my hands, and I quickly licked it off as I walked back to my father's place of employment. The guard didn't offer to take the pastry. Instead, he opened the door and nodded for me to enter.

My stomach dipped with excitement. To see inside the

house was something I'd never imagined. They catered only to male guests, and the only females allowed were those employed there. I kept my enthusiasm from my face as I stepped inside.

Soft music drifted down the halls along with the cloying smoke. My head began to spin as I walked down the dimly lit hall. A woman walked toward me. She wore only her grey facial veil, her heavy breasts with their dark nipples and thatch of hair between her legs visible for anyone who cared to look. I tried not to look but couldn't help myself. Even changing at home, my sisters and I gave each other privacy.

As my eyes swept her from head to toe, I noted she carried a cup. I moved aside as we neared, but she stopped and held out the cup to me. I hesitated to take it.

"Thank you, but I'm just here to bring my father, Mr. Hovtel, something to eat."

The woman laughed softly.

"I know, child. Drink the tea so the smoke doesn't bother you." She held out the cup again, but I didn't notice. The sound of her voice mesmerized me. It was so soft I had to strain to hear, and it had a sighing quality that hinted at a hidden yearning.

"How do you speak like that?" I asked, slipping into my father's world of observation and study. I was his daughter, after all.

She laughed again.

"After you feed your father, I will teach you if you'd like."

I nodded, accepted the cup, and drained it. Almost immediately, some of the spinning stopped. As it did, I realized I still stared at her breasts; and I quickly looked up to meet her eyes through her veil. I saw amusement there.

She took the cup back and led me down the hall. I couldn't help but watch her butt as she walked. Every move seemed slow and rolling, a smooth dance to call attention to different areas of her body. I felt no attraction, but curiosity bit into me deeply. No shame entered a single movement, even when she bent to stroke a cat that ambled down the hall, giving me a clear view of her...well, everything.

She surprised me by stopping suddenly in front of a door. She tapped on its surface instead of knocking, then opened it. She motioned me inside and followed me. Father sat at a desk, looking decidedly uncomfortable as he lectured on mathematics to four very naked and veiled students.

His voice seemed overly loud after the way my guide had spoken to me.

When he caught sight of me, his eyes widened in surprise, and I apologetically held out the pastry. He obviously didn't want me associating with his students for very visible reasons.

One of his students, who reclined before his desk, rose gracefully and took the pastry from me.

"I'll see you this evening," Father said, sounding strained.

I nodded and left without a word, my guide closing the door for me.

"Would you still like to learn, daughter of our teacher?" she whispered softly beside me.

I couldn't think of anything I wanted more at the moment, but I knew what my father would think. Or did I? As she pointed out, my father was a scholar. He, more than anyone I knew, understood what it meant to have a burning curiosity. Often he commended me on my tenacious pursuit of knowledge. Would he this time?

With resolve, I nodded. She led me to a set of stairs at the end of the current hallway. One led down, where I could hear gentle splashing sounds, and the other led up. Bright light and laughter spilled from the upstairs.

She hesitated at the landing.

"Perhaps it would be less shocking to go to the bathing room. It sounds as if most of my sisters are upstairs."

Without waiting for my answer, she glided down the candlelit steps which opened to a large underground room. Red dyed fabrics covered the rock walls, and large tubs filled with steaming water were placed throughout the room. An arched opening covered by another piece of red fabric led from the room.

A single woman, wearing the same style veil as my guide, occupied one of the many tubs.

"Good morning, sister," my guide whispered. "Are we disturbing you?"

"Not at all. Who is your friend? A new sister?"

My guide giggled, a tinkling sound that made me smile.

"Our scholar's curious daughter. She would like to know how we learned to speak like this."

"Come, sit near me. I would like to listen," the woman bade, standing to motion to the cushions set on the floor near the tub. Other than my father's chair, I hadn't noticed anything more than a cushion on which to sit. I sat next to my guide. The woman in the tub didn't sit until we sat, making it impossible to avoid seeing everything above the water that lapped at her knees. Her small nipples, rosy from the warm water, stood out from large breasts. No thatch of hair covered her lower parts or limbs.

"What is your name, child?" she asked, a smile curving her mouth. The veil fell to the top of her upper lip.

"Benella," I whispered back. I hadn't meant to whisper, at least not consciously. It just seemed too quiet and peaceful to speak regularly.

They both laughed lightly. The one in the tub introduced herself as Aryana and my guide as Ila.

"Why did you speak in a whisper?" Aryana asked.

"It feels wrong not to. Everything here is quiet and peaceful. I didn't want to disturb that."

Ila reached over and patted my arm with a smile.

"That is the heart of why we speak as we do. To bring peace to others, we must keep peace in ourselves at all times. We struggle; but when we do, we surround ourselves with our fellow sisters until peace returns. Speaking as we do comes with practice, but also deep peace."

"Drinking the tea every day doesn't hurt either," Aryana wryly interjected. "After prolonged drinking, the tea roughens our voices, making it uncomfortable to speak above a whisper. It also adds the husky quality that most find appealing."

"Ah," I said, feeling enlightened. Now that I had a little knowledge, I wanted more. "Why so many bathing tubs?"

They both laughed again.

"Definitely curious, this one," Aryana whispered with a wide smile. "Benella, the knowledge of this house is kept within the sisters and the clients we serve."

She didn't say it harshly, but I still felt embarrassed for assuming too much.

"I'm truly sorry. I meant no offense."

"Such a sweet girl," she said thoughtfully. "I can see you ask out of innocent curiosity, and I am willing to answer any questions you may have on one condition."

I nodded eagerly.

"You must never speak of what you learn here to

another person. If you can swear to that, I will tell you anything you like about our sisterhood."

Quickly swearing to her that I wouldn't dare speak of it —she laughed at that—she willingly explained about the tubs.

"We open our doors to our clients after ten in the morning. Many seek our comforts later in the evening. No matter when they seek us, we strive to have everything ready for them. Men are, by nature, aggressive and brash to some degree. Oh, women can be too, but we only serve men here so that is our focus. Their tendencies along with their strength can cause issues if we do not bring them peace quickly enough. The smoke helps as soon as they walk through the door. What the smoke cannot cleanse, a bath and body rub can."

I frowned slightly, recalling my bathing experiences. The feeling of warm water surrounding me certainly did have a calming effect, but the water cooled so quickly it didn't stay soothing for long. Frowning further, I recalled Father's tendencies to wash with cold water from a bucket. When he did require a full bath, we typically left the cottage for a walk, and when we returned, he already had everything cleaned up and back in place.

"Do men really enjoy bathing?"

Aryana smiled while Ila took a turn explaining.

"New clients do hesitate, but when they see one of us rise from the water, they are usually willing to join us."

"Oh." In my mind, the experience turned from cleaning to frolicking in the open. I eyed the other tubs in plain view of this one.

"Make no assumptions, Benella," Aryana said. "State your thoughts and ask your questions. I wouldn't like for you to leave with incorrect notions."

"Do you have sex with your clients in the tubs where everyone can see?" I asked bluntly and without censor.

Ila laughed loudly, a deep sound that had me looking at her with concern. Aryana chuckled.

"I will certainly tell the other sisters you evoked a true laugh from Ila. Something that hasn't been done in a long while."

I opened my mouth to ask how what I said was funny, but she cut me off.

"We do not pleasure our clients that way within the tubs. It would be a messy experience, and require more water changes and tub washing than time would permit." She rose from the water and stepped gracefully from the tub. Holding out a hand, she helped me to my feet.

"Come. We will show you."

We walked through the room toward the curtain. On the other side of the curtain, a large stove radiated heat. The adolescent boy tending the stove gave my dress a curious look but said nothing.

To the side of the boy, a square stone trough, about a foot deep, sunk into the floor.

"Here we heat the water we need and drain away the old water." Ila pointed to the hole in the bottom corner of the wall at the base of the trough. "When we bring a client to the bathing chambers, we walk him through the bathing chambers so he can see others enjoying the communal bath. This is especially important for a new client. The sight of the sisters naked and bathing inspires cooperation where there might otherwise exist hesitation or belligerence. In this room, we have the client stand in the trough and give him a cool water scrub. It initiates our time together and cleans him within and without so he is ready for the tubs."

"I'm not certain I understand," I said hesitantly. "How would this clean from within? Wouldn't the cool water wake the client from the smoke just a little and bring back some of his..." the word she'd used before slipped from my mind a moment. "Aggression?"

"Yes, it normally would. But a man craves a woman's touch. When we begin bathing him, the sister providing the bath becomes his focus. During this part of the bath, the sister helps release the man's pent energies."

Finally, understanding dawned, and the image of the baker frantically tugging at himself under his apron rose to mind. Something must have shown on my face because Aryana spoke gently beside me and laid a comforting hand on my arm.

"I see you understand, and it doesn't inspire pleasant

thoughts for you. What we do is not meant as an act of vulgarity but to bring peace."

"I understand. This interests me," I assured them. "Once a man has released his pent energies, then you move him to the tubs?"

Aryana gave me a relieved smile.

"If we are sharing too much information, please tell us. I would not offend our scholar's daughter on her first visit."

"Not too much information; just more than I've ever had before."

They both smiled knowingly and led me from the room. I could feel the boy's eyes on me as we walked away and wondered what things he saw in that room and why they allowed him there.

Ila continued the tour in the main bathing room.

"Since our clients only enter the waters clean, all we need do is keep the water warm and change it occasionally." She bent, again giving me a full view that I couldn't help but study, and pulled a large rock from the water.

I wondered what men thought when she did that.

"We heat these rocks by the stove and place them in the water throughout the day and night to keep the water warm."

The steam curling from the water called me to test it.

"May I?" I asked, stepping forward, pointing toward the water.

Ila nodded, and I dipped the tips of my fingers into the delightfully warm water.

"Oh, that is nice," I said.

"We do not have clients for a long while yet. We would be happy to send Gen away so you could bathe."

The tub we owned required a very uncomfortable position with my knees poking from the water. The beast's tub had been just as big as these, enough to fit two, but I hadn't been able to enjoy it. If they sent the boy away, I had no doubt I could have a real, uninterrupted bath.

"I..." I wanted to say yes, but what if I misunderstood and they required payment for the use of the bath. Accepting things from the beast had caused me trouble.

"Perhaps another time."

Aryana tilted her head.

"You wanted to say yes. What stopped you?"

"What do you want in return?"

"Nothing at all. We enjoy the company of other women. As a sister, we usually only speak with other sisters. Not many other women are willing to speak with us."

"Then I would greatly appreciate it. Though, I'm not sure my father would like it. I would prefer no one mention my extended visit unless he specifically asks." I wouldn't ask them to lie.

"We understand," Aryana said as Ila calmly led the way to the back bathing room.

While Aryana spoke to Gen, Ila quickly explained what I should do. Once they all left, I stripped to nothing, draped my clothes on the pegs lining the wall, and stepped into the trough.

Using the buckets nearby, I wet my skin then used the special scented soap that Aryana had brought down for her own bath. The light, sweet smell made my stomach rumble, reminding me that I hadn't yet eaten. I lathered my hair, enjoying the heat from the stove as I stood there covered in nothing but suds. Then I tilted the first bucket over my head, slowly rinsing it all away. As they directed, I used the second bucket to ensure I missed nothing.

Nervous, I peeked around the curtain before tiptoeing out and sliding into the first tub with a gusty sigh. The water stung my skin with its heat, but in a good way. I melted against the edge, sinking until my chin hit the water. Delightfully, my knees stayed submerged, too. My eyes fluttered closed.

"Benella," Aryana's now familiar whisper drifted to me. "May we sit on the cushions by you while you relax?"

I opened my eyes and nodded easily. These women strove to bring a sense of calm to everyone they encountered. I knew they would do nothing to intentionally disrupt that. And after the way they moved around me, I felt comfortable enough with my submerged nudity to talk to them without shame.

Ila glided into the room with her, and they both sank to the cushions.

"We just replaced the rocks in the tubs. You don't find it too hot?" Aryana asked.

I shook my head lazily with a slight smile. She reached over the tub and tested the water.

"It would be best to only sit in it for a few minutes then move to one of the cooler tubs. Too long in the heat could make you ill," she cautioned.

"You have very pretty hair, Benella," Ila whispered, reaching out to touch the wet strands hanging over the edge of the tub. "Would you mind if I oiled it and brushed it?"

Mind? I vaguely recalled my mother doing that when I was young; but after that, I'd struggled with my own hair, often tearing through tangles to braid it without combing it.

"I wouldn't mind," I assured her. She stood smoothly, left the room, and walked upstairs.

"Come." Aryana stood. "Let's move you to a cooler tub before she returns. You're looking too red in the face." She held out her hand, and I hesitated. "I promise you, I've seen all manner of parts on my sisters, and yours are no different."

They might not be so different, but they were parts never seen before by anyone. She was right about the water, though. I could feel sweat beading my upper lip.

"Maybe another rinse bucket would be beneficial before going to another tub," I suggested, accepting her hand.

I stood and avoided meeting her gaze or moving too quickly. Everything they did was slow and measured. I didn't want to do anything they would consider aggressive or manly. I wondered what they would think if they knew I often wore trousers and a shirt. Inside, I laughed at the thought. They probably wouldn't say anything. They wore nothing, after all.

As I stepped into the trough, Aryana spoke.

"You are very beautiful, Benella, and when you fully realize that, I pity the men in your path."

The sincerity in her tone had me raising my eyes. She gave me a gentle smile then bent to pick up the rinse bucket.

"Ready?" she asked with the bucket poised over her head, her breasts lifted high, their rosy peaks taunting me with my own inadequacies.

I didn't think of myself as unattractive, just unendowed. Everyone else sported nice round breasts while mine seemed a bit smallish.

"Ready," I whispered.

The cool water rushed over my head, putting out a fire I hadn't noticed. I sighed in relief, and she laughed.

"I thought you looked too warm. Come, you still have time to relax while we oil your hair."

CHAPTER NINE

LONG BEFORE THE FIRST CLIENT STEPPED THROUGH the door of the Whispering Sisters, I found myself walking toward the estate's gate. After leaving the sisters, I'd known I couldn't go home. My hair smelled too nice for Bryn not to notice and start asking questions that I didn't want to answer. Father didn't like me knowing where he worked; I could only imagine how he would feel if two of his daughters knew.

If not for my growling stomach and the lack of food and coin at home, I wouldn't have come. The beast hadn't expected me today, and I wasn't sure of my unplanned welcome.

Standing inside the gate, waiting for the gathering mist that heralded the beast, I reflected on the new friends I had made. They'd taught me so much in a short period of time. When I'd left, they'd invited me to return any day before ten for another visit. I knew I would return. Their veils begged to be questioned.

"You have returned," he said.

I smiled slightly at his puzzled tone.

"I hope you don't mind. Do you have work for me? I'm really hungry."

The barest scrape of his foot on the ground behind me warned me where he stood. I'd grown so used to his cloaked presence that I felt no fear, just uncertainty. Perhaps the relaxing morning had something to do with my mood as well.

His hand touched my hair, and I heard him inhale deeply.

"No cleaning the kitchen today." His voice clicked with agitation. "Do you read?"

The question surprised me.

"Yes."

"The pages often tear when I try to turn them. Today, you will read for me. Come."

He led the way to the estate, his outline always just on the edge of my vision. We entered through the kitchen door. The mist swallowed all of the light indoors.

"I cannot see," I said. Hearing my own whispering voice, I wondered if I should try speaking softly to the beast. Perhaps he might growl less.

"Take my tail," he said with an agitated growl.

Something thick and heavy whacked against my side. I

reached out and curled a hand around his thick, furry tail. He waited a moment before moving, walking slowly so I could keep pace without tugging on his appendage. While we walked, I couldn't help but bring my other hand to his tail to touch the coarse fur. When he'd carried me, I'd been too hurt to notice his fur, and I couldn't recall much detail from when I'd slept on it.

I spread my fingers and delved into his fur, stroking it the wrong way so the hair tickled between my fingers. Changing directions, I smoothed it back down. He neither growled nor spoke, so I continued with my touch as we wound through black hallways until we entered a large muffled room. We walked several steps in, and then he stopped. Reluctantly, I released his tail. It felt like the first semi-friendly touch we'd shared where my role involved more than holding still.

"Light a candle and sit facing away from the door," he said with a deep growl. "I will return shortly."

He left, taking the mist with him. A sliver of light shone straight ahead, and I cautiously shuffled toward it. Heavy drapery met my touch, and I tentatively pushed it aside. The large, glass-paned window framed a beautiful view of a very overgrown yard.

My mouth dropped open as a tree—of sorts—scampered into view. Its white paper skin marked with black dots and raised lines reminded me of a birch's bark. The fingers on her hands and the toes on her feet sprouted with leaves. Where hair should have streamed down her back, a cascade of wisp thin branches, heavily adorned with bright green spring leaves, grew instead. Her form looked very human, including two lumps on her main trunk to indicate breasts. A tree nymph.

Enthralled, I watched her spin and look over her shoulder with a smile. Another nymph came into view, this one obviously male, based on the short thick branch that extended from the area just above where the main trunk split into something resembling human legs.

The male nymph caught up to the female and spun her to face him. She tilted her head back with a wide smile, her leaf hair catching the light prettily. He grasped her behind the knee with one hand and drew her leg up over his hip. Between them, I could see his jutting root. The leg he had lifted melted into his trunk, solidifying the two into one. Slowly, he flexed forward, and I watched the root disappear. The scene left me warm as if I still sat in the hot waters at the Whispering Sisters. The male withdrew and flexed forward again. Both seemed to be enjoying it very much, and I felt a twinge of shame for watching.

Prying my fingers one by one from the curtain, I was about to let it drop when a dark mist came rolling in from the left. The male's head shot up, turning unnaturally to look at the mist. When he saw it, he broke away from his partner and immediately solidified into a tree.

The female, however, did not solidify. Instead, with a

small smile, she glanced at the mist, then bent forward. The position brought to memory—in vivid detail—how Ila had looked when she bent to pet the cat. The mist consumed the back half of the nymph, pouring over her like an angry wave. Bent forward as she was, I watched the nymph's leaf hair sway as something pushed against her again and again.

Carefully, I let the curtain fall, hoping it wouldn't draw the attention of any of the parties outside, and scrambled to find a candle and a book. I flopped onto a sofa, kicking my feet up in a relaxed pose, just as I heard the beast enter the room.

"What book did you choose?" he asked softly, with only a hint of a growl. His hand found my hair and gently tugged it out so he could stroke it. I could smell a hint of outdoors on him.

I couldn't find my voice to speak. Lifting the book, I showed him the cover. I stared at it, too. A book on farming. My already thumping heart beat harder. Would he know now that I had seen them?

"This will be an enlightening hour," he said, and I felt him settle on the floor by my head, his hands still running through my hair. He breathed in deeply again, and I knew he was smelling the oil Ila had rubbed into the strands.

"Proceed."

After clearing my throat, I began to speak softly about a farmer's woes and how to alleviate them.

MORE THAN AN HOUR passed before I set the book on my chest. What most would find boring had interested me to the point that I'd forgotten the time and the hands running through my hair. When I ceased reading, the beast halted as well.

"Why have you stopped?" he demanded in a growl.

"I haven't had anything to eat today and am thirsty," I said softly.

He grunted his objection, but I heard him stand.

"Can I hold your tail again?" I asked, thinking of the dark halls.

The mist in the room suddenly churned so darkly it extinguished the candle. I recalled the scene outside the window and regretted my request. I sat up in concern and tentatively reached out a hand. Almost immediately, I connected with fur, more than I could wrap a hand around. Unsure what else to do, I trailed my fingers along the fur until I understood I touched his hip. I carefully trailed my hand further back and clasped his tail.

Through it all, he held still and said nothing. I whispered a quick apology. He began walking, and this time, I didn't do more than hold his tail.

A few minutes later, we stepped into the kitchen.

"There is a tray on the block for you. Will you read more to me after you eat?" he asked impatiently.

"Yes," I whispered, trying to emulate the sisters to help calm him.

"Then, I will return shortly," he said, anger clipping his words.

"Wait," I called before the mist left. "I would rather eat in the library if you don't mind."

I'd noticed the number of books that lined the walls of the library when I'd raced to grab a book earlier. I wanted a chance to explore that space.

"Of course." The clicking quality was back in his voice.

I carried the tray in one hand while holding his tail in the other. He had barely stepped into the library when his tail tugged from my grasp. As he left, the candle flared to life so I could see. I sighed and set the tray down.

Curiously, I peeked out the window to see if the nymphs had resumed their frolic. To my surprise, the male remained frozen in the same position. The female sat at his feet, idly touching his root, which no longer stood out stiffly. I felt pity for her. Obviously, the interruption to their play had upset her partner.

As before, a black mist roiled in from the left, catching my attention. The female nymph stood slowly with a lingering sad touch on her partner before backing away a few steps. She didn't look as eager this time as she bent forward.

The mist rolled over her. In its depths, I discerned the shadow of the beast as he reared back on his hind legs. He braced his hands on her back and thrust forward into the nymph. He drove into her tirelessly, and I wondered how she stayed upright, until I noticed her feet rooted into the ground.

Troubled, I let the curtain fall. The enchantments on this place were a puzzle to me, often not appearing to adhere to any rules, such as the food that grew outside the wall. Now, I wondered if there were rules to the creatures here. Why hadn't the female nymph solidified into a tree to escape the beast? She hadn't appeared to want the beast's attention this time. Yet, instead of solidifying, she had rooted her feet in order to accommodate him. Why?

While I pondered possible reasons for what I'd witnessed, I went to my food and drink. Before the beast returned, I'd drunk my fill, eaten a bit of cheese, and then stored the rest of it in my bag to share with Father in the morning.

When the beast entered the room, I was exploring a small section of books.

"Continue," he prompted me softly, again with barely a growl.

I cautiously returned to the lounge, noting from my peripheral that no shadowy mist followed him.

Pent energies, I thought as I began to read. The beast seemed to have a lot of them. I knew the basics of the act I'd seen performed—after all, I'd discovered Bryn doing the same—but some of the finer details I'd yet to puzzle out.

For instance, why a woman would want to do that? Obviously, the male enjoyed it. I recalled Sara's reaction to the baker and Bryn's noises. Both women made those noises from what I thought came from enjoyment; but afterward, both had been sad.

I read for a while longer before closing the book softly. The beast's fingers stilled in my hair.

I remained prone on the sofa, quietly thinking. He willingly traded my time for food, and he didn't seem to care how I spent that time so long as it was in his manor. If he truly wanted it cleaned, he would not have asked for me to read. Likewise, if he wanted to hear another's voice, he would have asked me to read from the beginning. Everything seemed to be on a whim with him, even his frolic with the nymph. Yet, each time I fulfilled my time obligation, he asked the same question and became agitated when I took my leave.

"Sir, why do you keep asking me to return?"

"That is my concern," he growled.

"It seems my visits cause you more anger than peace. Perhaps I shouldn't return," I said softly.

"No," he said with a harsh growl before sucking in a great breath. Slowly, the breath eased out. "I apologize for my anger. Return tomorrow, please."

"Will I clean tomorrow?" I asked tentatively. "I enjoy reading, but would like to earn more food to take home with me."

"You will leave with food today," he snarled at me as the mist swirled into the room and extinguished the candle again.

His tail bumped my neck, and I stood with my hand wrapped lightly around it.

I didn't understand his mercurial temper. Perhaps it was just his nature.

When we arrived in the kitchen, he stormed out the door without a word. On the block, I found a variety of cheeses and bread, which I stuffed into my bag.

THE NEXT MORNING, I waited until Father left before rising from bed. We hadn't discussed where he worked, yet, or that I'd brought him breakfast twice. I decided I would do the same for him, again, since I hadn't purchased oats with the coin I'd received in trade for a wheel of hard cheese. I had been given a full high silver. Twice the value of a blunt silver. I'd never held so much at once and honestly didn't know what to do with it. I'd slept with it tucked into my bindings.

When I arrived at the back door of the Whispering Sisters not much later, carrying a glazed pastry, I had a blunt silver and eighteen coppers still in my bag. The baker hadn't fussed about making change for a high silver, apparently having plenty of his own.

The guard at the door nodded and held the door for me to enter. I smiled and went inside, the smoke swamping my head almost immediately. However, Ila was waiting in the hallway with a cup of tea.

"How did you know I was coming?" I asked, after draining it.

"We watch from our windows. Another sister spotted you and let me know."

I delivered the pastry to my very surprised father who asked to speak with me in the hallway. Ila excused herself and stepped inside to speak with one of her sisters.

"I would prefer—"

I stopped him with a raised hand.

"You've raised me, taught me, and uprooted our family to protect me. Let me bring you breakfast when you forget to eat."

His shoulders slumped in defeat, and he nodded.

"I like the sisters," I said so softly that he had to lean forward to hear. "But you should rest easy when I'm here. Their life does not call to me."

He met my eyes with relief and gave me a brief hug to which the population of the room softly aw'ed, embarrassing him. I smiled at him as Ila joined me and closed the door. We retreated to the bathing room by an unspoken agreement.

"I can see the questions running through your mind," she said as we descended.

"Yes, but they aren't necessarily about the sisters," I admitted. "We've touched a little on the mood of men. What do you do with an angry man?"

"You want to know what we do, or would like advice regarding how you should handle an angry man?" Aryana asked, rising from the water in one of the tubs. She stepped over the edge and motioned to the back room.

Absently, I licked the glaze from my fingers as we moved. I didn't want anyone knowing about the beast nor did I want their questions if I admitted to having to deal with an angry man.

"What you would do."

Ila waved Gen from the room as she stepped into the trough and gave Aryana a concerned look. Aryana sluiced water over Ila and handed her soap without acknowledging the look.

"When our clients leave the baths, some choose to follow us upstairs for muscle relief." They worked together to lather Ila's body, using languid strokes. I would have felt uncomfortable, but neither seemed aware of the other's touch as they remained focused on me.

"Many who visit us do physical labor that leaves them sore and strained," Aryana continued, absently smoothing her hand over Ila's right breast and leaving a soap trail. "A man with pain is more likely quick to temper. We can show you our techniques, but you must promise never to use them."

I eagerly agreed. The beast didn't seem to do physical labor, so I didn't think the information would benefit him, but I always sought to learn new things. Learning this could lead to other things that might eventually lead to knowledge that could help control the beast's temper.

Ila frowned while sliding her hand between her legs to wash her lower parts.

"Are you sure that's wise?"

Aryana helped her rinse.

"Better to have understanding of a room in the light before trying to walk about it in the dark."

Ila nodded and took a moment to stand before the stove to dry.

Aryana's remark made sense. What they had to teach probably bordered on inappropriate, but knowledge made choices easier. If I knew what obstacles to watch for, I wouldn't trip on them.

Aryana led the way upstairs to a room where Gen lounged on a flat sofa with no back. He didn't seem surprised when we entered.

"Gen, would you mind being our display for a skin and muscle touch?"

The adolescent, around my age, shrugged and nodded, but remained sitting.

Ila took me by the hand and led me back into the hall where we waited. "There are many aspects to a man. For you to fully understand them, we need to show you some of the dangers you might innocently overlook."

"What do you mean?" I asked, confused.

Aryana called softly from within the room, and Ila smiled.

"You will see."

When we walked back in, Gen lay on the sofa on his stomach with a light sheet over his head. Aryana caught my curious look.

"Just as we veil our faces to keep the focus on our bodies and our clients' needs, we must cover Gen's face to keep our focus on his body and our explanation. Gen's body, not his face, will tell us his needs."

Interesting, I thought, stepping closer. Gen still had the thin wiry muscles of youth, and I enjoyed looking at him.

"If releasing the pent energies does not remove a man's anger, we look at his body as a whole. Tension, which can cause anger, can be carried in many places throughout the body," Ila began her explanation, running her hand lightly over Gen's back and down his leg to the sole of his foot. She then ran her hand the opposite direction on the opposite side.

She explained the placement of certain muscles and what kind of touch to use to soothe the tension from them. When she'd covered the back of him, including the muscles of his butt, she asked him to flip over. She was careful to keep his face covered.

Immediately, my eyes drifted to his penis, and I thought of the poor wood nymph's wilted root. Gen's penis lay relaxed against the tangle of hair surrounding it. Under it hung a large sac with two obvious lumps. Ila chuckled at my long stare and gave me the names of each. I knew the term penis, thanks to one of my father's medicinal books, but ballsack was new and sounded odd.

Aryana took over the instruction of the front, starting with the arms and legs, then going to the chest. Their explanation of the tissue beneath the surface fascinated me, and I wondered if Father would be as interested.

"The soft area of the stomach, below the ribs and above the hips, should not be touched using any of the techniques we've shown you so far," Aryana said, trailing her fingers lightly over the skin.

I noticed Gen's penis twitch again as it had occasionally since he'd turned to his stomach.

"A man's rod will often respond with the use of any of these techniques; and that is what you must watch for because, instead of relaxing him, you may be causing an increase in pent energies."

She slid her hand over his stomach again in a firmer touch and trailed over the crease of his thigh. His penis jumped significantly. She trailed her hand lightly over his ballsack, and I watched in fascination as his penis stood upright.

"If it gets to this point, you can be assured, you are in trouble and should leave quickly before he becomes of a mind to have *you* release his pent energies for him."

She grasped Gen's penis firmly, and I watched the head of it turn red. Ila took a small vial from a nearby shelf and drizzled oil over the tip, which Aryana smoothed down its length. Then, she proceeded to stroke it in a smooth, slow rhythm. I couldn't look away.

Gen began to twitch slightly on the sofa, his hips thrusting forward to meet her downward slide. The room grew warm for me. The sac, which had been loose before, began to tighten and shrink. Aryana stopped, abruptly releasing his penis and stepping back. Ila used a gentle arm to nudge me back as well and motioned me to remain silent.

"Aryana," Gen rasped from under the sheet, his hips bucking forward. When she didn't answer, he bolted upright, whipping off the sheet from his face. He angrily glared at Aryana and Ila.

"I did not agree to this," he ground out, his face flushed.

Aryana held up both hands.

"A few moments more of your patience, Gen, might save our dear Benella from terrible mistakes," she said softly.

His eyes narrowed, but he nodded and lay back down, curling his own hand around his penis. He didn't stroke it as Aryana had. He held it as one would a bruised appendage.

"If a man's energies are pent and not released, he will become volatile, unpredictable. Tension will creep into his body and often stay there even after the energies are eventually released. If you touch a man, no matter how innocent the touch, watch for the signs," Aryana warned. "Be sure your touch is only releasing tension and not building pent energies."

Fascinated, I nodded my understanding. It did sound a bit like the beast. Even after his encounter with the wood nymph and he'd released his energies, he had still kept his tension. The sisters were right about the dangers. I would never attempt anything like what I'd just learned on the beast. I feared his response.

"Come," Ila whispered, taking my hand. "Some mysteries we will leave you to discover on your own."

She led me from the room as Aryana gently removed Gen's hand and replaced it with her own. Before we reached the end of the hall, I heard his loud groan.

THE DARK, rolling mist waited beyond the groaning gate of

the estate. I calmly stepped into the shadows and walked forward until the gate closed behind me.

"What would you have me clean today?" I asked softly.

"The servant's quarters in the kitchen in exchange for as many berries as you can carry," he said in his typical aggravated tone.

"Lead the way."

In the kitchen, he left me to work, darkening the room occasionally to watch me after I'd changed from my dress.

The chairs stood in good repair, and a new table had taken the place of the damaged one. I dragged half of the broken table outside and tugged the mattresses out, one by one, for an airing. I even scoured the floor in the room and washed the window.

When I finished, I changed and wandered back into the kitchen to find food on the new table along with my bag filled with berries wrapped in two layers of soft cloth. No doubt, many would be crushed before I returned to the Water.

I ate my fill of bread, quail, and squash, then shouldered my bag. As soon as I moved toward the door, the beast returned in his shrouding mists.

"Will you stay?" he asked.

"I cannot."

He left in a fit of anger, and I found my own way to the gate. As I predicted, some of the berries did not survive the journey. Crushed by the weight of other berries, they bled through the cloth, my bag, and into my dress near the hip.

When I reached the bridge, a cooler wind gusted from the north and clouds drifted over the sun. The berries I carried would need either to be dried or eaten before they spoiled. Without the sun to help, drying would prove too difficult. I wandered to the market district and traded oats for berries.

Bryn was within the cottage, cooking dinner when I returned with the remaining berries and the small portion of oats. I let her know they were for Father when I set them down. She nodded and coughed lightly into her apron before telling me dinner had another twenty minutes.

Sitting in Father's chair, I perused a book, listening to the scrape of the spoon on the pan and the occasional light cough while thinking about the beast.

Perhaps tomorrow I should bargain my time for answers instead of food.

THE NEXT MORNING, Father remained near Bryn's bedside instead of leaving for the Whispering Sisters. During the night, her light cough had turned into a deep, grating whoop of air. None of us slept well from dusk to light, and nothing Father tried worked.

Dressing quickly in my stained dress, I took the coins

I'd saved and ran to the business district to knock on the doors of anyone boasting knowledge of medicine. I finally found a learned doctor who claimed knowledge of the illness as well as a remedy. It took all of the coins I had to convince him to follow me home.

Bryn still lay in bed, rasping for breath when we arrived. The doctor asked Father to leave the room while he examined her. He cautioned Blye, who was already dressed for work, to remain until he concluded his exam. Several minutes later, he exited the bedroom.

"You should all remain in quarantine until this passes. Here is the medicine you will need once you start to cough. Take one dose a day. If you run out, I have more for purchase."

He and Father spoke quietly for several minutes before the doctor took his leave.

Father sat heavily in the chair before the fire.

"Blye, there is only enough medicine for three, should we all become sick. Do you have coin for another bottle?"

"I purchased cloth with the coin I had and am making my own dresses for the shop to sell. I have nothing until I finish them," she said with a worried quaver.

"Benella?"

I shook my head.

"I gave the doctor everything I had to get him here."

"He is going to tell the Head, and they will place us under mandatory quarantine. Take your bag and leave.

Forage for what you can to trade should we need it. Go," he said sharply.

Grabbing my bag, I flew out the door, not arguing with the fault in his logic. If we were to be quarantined, no one would want to trade with me for anything I found. The whole point was not to spread the sickness.

Dark, heavy clouds hung damp in the sky, casting gloom over the town. I raced lightly to the Whispering Sisters and called to the guard that Bryn was ill and Father would not return until she recovered. I asked him to discreetly let Blye's seamstress know, too.

He nodded, and I spun away in a hurry to leave the Water behind me.

CHAPTER TEN

On the outskirts of the estate, the sky rumbled and let loose a torrent of cold, spring rain to pound the ground. I sloshed the remaining distance to the gate, disheartened to see it raining inside, too. I'd hoped the magic would keep it out and let me dry.

No mist waited for me, so I found my own way to the manor, shivering as I let myself into the kitchen. A small fire crackled in the hearth, and I eagerly closed the door on the poor weather. Disregarding the trail of water I left, I crossed the room to warm myself. The heat from the flames barely heated my fingers and did nothing to reduce my trembling. Only dry clothes would warm me.

My boots made squishing noises as I walked to the servant's quarters. I closed the door, then struggled to remove my dress. Peeling off the wet mass wasn't easy. Shivering, I dug in my sodden bag for my shirt and trousers. The pants were soaked, but the shirt had escaped most of the water and only felt damp. I removed my wet binding, laid it over the footboard of the bed, and tugged on the shirt.

Sitting on the edge of the bed, I removed my boots and socks. The cold floor further numbed my feet while I gathered up my dress and pants. With my wet clothes draped over one arm and my boots in my hand, I opened the door to a mist filled kitchen. It was so dark the light of the fire didn't penetrate more than a few feet into the gloom.

"I didn't expect you so soon," the beast rumbled from the darkness.

Holding my dress to shield my bare legs, I hesitated in the doorway and debated if I should retreat into the room until I dried.

"My sister is sick. Father sent me to gather what I could to trade for more medicine. We were all told to stay in quarantine, so you might not want to come too close." I was less concerned about spreading sickness to an enchanted creature than I was about tempting the beast.

"There is washing to be done. Follow me, and I will show you to the laundry."

The fire snuffed out, and his tail bumped against me. I had no choice but to drop my boots and walk across the cold stone floor, holding his tail so I could follow.

It seemed that the winding path led behind the

kitchen. Rain pinged against a window, and the sound echoed in the room. I continued to hold onto the beast's tail, unable to see anything.

"Stand here," he said gruffly as his tail pulled from my grasp.

In a moment, a fire burst to life on each end of the room, flooding the large area with light. At the opposite side of the room, two windows marked the wall with a door that led outside. Near the door, three wooden half-barrels squatted heavily beside the fireplace. Not far from there, a long table abutted the wall and racks for drying lay in a tumble. In order to wash anything, I would need to right the drying racks and fill the tubs. Both tasks requiring more bending than I would want to perform when dressed only in a shirt.

Turning, I eyed the mist just outside the arched entry I'd come through.

"May I have something to drink, sir?"

The mist receded, and I sagged with relief. I quickly tossed my dress over a drying rack and moved the rest of the racks into place between the tubs and the arch. To the left of the back door, lay a pile of dirty linens. By arranging several of those over the drying racks, I created a screen for myself before setting to work.

A large kettle and a cistern to the right of the fire gave me what I needed to start the process. The beast returned while I sorted through the soiled pile, his clicking growl announcing his presence. Arms around a mound of linens, I didn't turn to acknowledge him as I dropped everything into an empty tub.

The growling faded as I tested the heating water, so I braved looking around. A clay pitcher and a stout cup had appeared on the long back table. Cautiously, I tiptoed from behind my screens and poured myself some water. My throat felt dry and slightly sore, probably from walking in the rain. The cool water soothed it enough that I could focus on laundry.

It took a long time to fill the tub with hot water and even longer to scrub soap into the cloth. The soapy steam tickled my throat enough that I coughed occasionally. While I let the cloth soak, I filled another tub with cool water for rinsing. The heat from both fires warmed the room so much that I had to wipe the sweat from my brow. I no longer felt the chill from the floor.

Coughing made my throat sore, which made me cough more as I rinsed and wrung out the water. I changed the material screening me from the dirty ones to the clean ones and washed the second tub of linens.

A mist invaded the room again while I worked, easily two hours after I had started. He made no noise, not even a growl. I felt his eyes following me as I moved from the washtub to the rinse tub. As I twisted the material, sweating and coughing, I realized I would need to walk from my screen to hang the second string of bedding. But, the shirt I wore only hung to the tops of my thighs. As I considered the situation, I decided I didn't care as much anymore. I was hot and tired and wanted to finish, return home, and go to bed. With that thought, I realized I had Bryn's ailment.

Stepping from around the screens, I coughed harder and heard a slight wheeze as I inhaled. Yet, I continued to drape wet linens over a drying rack along with several shirts with torn button holes and missing buttons that I had found and washed. As soon as I deposited the last piece, I touched my still damp dress and looked toward the arch.

"Finished," I said softly.

Outside, the rain continued to pound against the door, so it didn't matter if the dress was dry. But would I make it home? Bryn had grown gradually worse in a short period of time.

"Will you accept my offer?" he asked.

"What exactly is your offer?" I asked. The heat I felt no longer came from the fires, but from inside.

"Stay with me, do as I command, and I will grant your every wish."

"And my family? Will I see them?"

He growled fiercely, giving me the answer I'd already known.

"I cannot accept your offer." A cough ripped from me, and I struggled to catch my breath. "But I don't think I can leave yet, either. May I stay in the servant's quarters until the rain stops?"

The mist swirled around me, blocking all light from the fires. His hand brushed my brow lightly, the touch brief. Suddenly, he bumped into me, knocking me into his arms.

"You may stay until you are well."

With him carrying me, we flew through the halls to the kitchen. He gently set me on one of the bare mattresses and left in a whirl. I shivered in the cool room, coughing so hard my stomach hurt. He returned with a thick comforter and covered me gently. I closed my eyes and asked for one more thing.

"Please send word to my father. I don't want him to worry."

HEAT BURNED THROUGH ME, and a crow cawed loudly. Wind roared through the room, making the beds shake. From the shadows a demon rose. Black with glowing red eyes, it opened its massive maw and bit down into my chest, opening me wide and tearing me apart with each cough. I faded.

"HELP HER!"

The roar filled the room, a distraction from the painful cough consuming me.

"Are you willing to pay the price?" a voice demanded sharply, sounding vaguely familiar.

"Wretched woman, haven't I given you enough? What more would you take from me?"

"Secrecy. Before she leaves, you must reveal yourself," the voice said in an angry, spiteful tone. "No mist to hide you. You deserve no respite. You've learned nothing."

A moment of silence reigned while the demon continued to devour me.

"Yes, I will pay the price and wish you to hell," he said raggedly.

"Here, give her one dose of this each day until she is well. Now, don't bother me again unless it's to give me what I want."

A cold wind rushed through the room, then a large hand burrowed under my head to lift me slightly. A cup pressed to my lips and liquid touched them. I swallowed convulsively three times before the hand lowered me to the mattress again. The liquid flowed down, burning through the wounds the demon had chewed, until I cried and begged for help.

The beast whispered promises in my ear. He asked me to give him my obedience, and he would stop the demon's feasting. I thought of my father and, hoping he didn't suffer the same fate, shook my head to deny the beast. The bed trembled with his anger.

THE DEMON LEFT at some point during the night, but the wounds he'd caused remained to fester and boil. Again, the beast lifted my head and forced me to drink the vile draught of water and medicine. It didn't burn as much when I coughed afterward.

He continued to whisper in my ear as I drifted in and out of sleep, making outrageous promises in return for my word to remain with him forever. His insistency didn't make any sense to me, and I shook my head to deny him each time.

WHEN I OPENED my eyes the following morning, I groaned at the sunlight streaming through the single window and wished I hadn't cleaned the glass so well. I coughed lightly and remembered the dreams I had of a creature ravaging my chest. Licking my dry lips, I turned my head to look around the room and found that I was alone and the door to the room closed.

I struggled upright and managed to bring myself to a sitting position. My bladder needed relief, and a chamber pot sat in the corner. The cold floor abraded my suddenly sensitive feet as I shuffled toward the pot. The shirt that I'd worn made it easier to do what needed to be done and get back into bed.

As soon as I pulled the cover over me again, the door crashed open and the dark mist rolled into the room.

"How long have I been ill?" I asked, not caring about courtesy.

"This is the second day," he said, sliding a hand under my head and forcing me to drain a cup of plain water. It sat cold and heavy in my stomach in a good way.

I felt sleep pulling at me.

"Did you send word to my father?" I asked.

"Yes. He knows you are safe and being cared for." His fingers touched my hair, and my eyes fluttered closed.

I slept several hours before waking again. The light through the window didn't shine as brightly. A chair near the bed held a cup filled with water. I reached for it eagerly and drained it before making another visit to the chamber pot.

My limbs shook less, but sleep still pulled at me. Again, when I returned to the bed, the beast reappeared in his masking mist.

"Are you feeling well enough to leave?" he asked angrily.

The thought of trudging home made me wince.

"If possible, I would leave and not exhaust your

hospitality, but I'm afraid I wouldn't make it very far," I said, wondering if he would insist I leave regardless.

"Very well," he said, seemingly mollified. "Another night then, unless you'd rather stay indefinitely. There are many rooms much more suited to a permanent guest."

I opened my mouth to deny him, but he continued.

"Beds soft enough to sink several inches and drapes thick enough to keep away the deepest winter's chill. And wardrobes filled with dresses of supple cloth to caress your skin. You would want for nothing," he assured me.

"Why are you so desperate to keep me here?" I asked.

"Why do you refuse me so insistently?" he countered with a growl.

"Because you've given me no reason to stay," I said without meaning to. Perhaps being ill prevented my good sense from filtering what came out of my mouth. "You don't know anything about me. Now, tell me why you want me to stay."

He roared loudly, during which I caught a curse on all women, then he left in a fury. He slammed the door so hard it tore from the hinges and fell flat to the floor. I was glad the chamber pot wasn't near it. It would have been a mess to clean up.

I rolled to my side, facing the door, and noticed a tray with bread and a bowl of broth on the chair. Guilt swamped me for aggravating him so much when he'd obviously been taking care of me. I ate the bread, dipping it in the broth, while I tried to arrive at a reasonable explanation for his insistence that I stay.

Though he'd always seemed angry, he did provide for me. Yet, the night I'd run from Tennen and the vines pulled me to the estate—the night the beast had asked to see me naked—made me doubt that his care was due to compassion. However, since then, he'd asked of nothing improper from me, only that I clean...and one time that I read to him. Could he just be lonely?

What about the other enchanted creatures, though? And the old woman he'd brought me to when I'd hit my head on the pole? I recalled the conversation I'd heard while dreaming of the flesh-eating demon. Though I knew the demon was only a product of my fevered mind, I felt that conversation had been real. She'd given him the medicine I needed, and he had promised something in return.

The beast truly did provide for me. But why? I fell asleep before I could arrive at any conclusion.

When I woke next, I heard the crackle of a fire from the kitchen and noticed its soft glow illuminating the floor where the door had lain. Someone had removed the door while I slept. My stomach rumbled, and I looked to the chair, hoping for more broth. Instead, a gown draped over the back of it. The dress had more ruffles than I cared for, but I knew the beast meant for me to wear it as an example of what he could offer.

I pulled myself upright and quickly shed the shirt to tug on the dress. It fit snuggly, its supple material clinging and caressing my skin as he promised. When I stood, it fell to the floor in an overabundant cascade. It brought back memories of trying to run through the woods with Tennen right behind me.

Trying not to scowl, I treaded lightly to the kitchen. A crisp, white linen covered the new table. A feast lay out upon it, and the smells of roasted fowl, creamed soups, baked vegetables, and warm bread perfumed the air. Forgetting the dress, I moved to the only setting at the table and pushed back my chair, kicking my skirt slightly to move it out of the way as I sat.

Picking up the fork, I didn't hesitate to start eating. Everything looked and smelled so good my mouth watered with anticipation.

I didn't realize the beast had drifted into the room until he passed before the fire and momentarily blocked the light.

"Are you pleased?" he asked.

"The food is delicious. Thank you," I said after swallowing a bite. I broke off a hunk of steaming bread and smeared soft butter on it. My eyes rolled back.

"And the dress?" he asked.

"Suitably ruffled for such a fine meal," I said.

"Have you given my offer further consideration?"

Letting silence fall as I chewed a large bite, I wondered how to answer his question. Had I thought on his offer? Yes, but only to try to determine why he repeatedly asked, not to give it serious consideration. After all, I knew nothing of significance regarding the beast to give his proposal serious thought.

"Do you want to know why I consistently say no?" I didn't wait for him to respond. "How can I offer to stay, to obey your commands, when I see the considerable amount of cruelty and anger in you? How will you turn that on me when I am yours to command?" He growled ominously but didn't move closer to the table.

"You know nothing of my anger." A warning growl coated his words.

"I know that you resent this manor and would have gladly ripped it down if the magic here would have let you. And I know that you disregard most of the creatures here with you."

"Ridiculous," he roared. "I do not disregard those trapped here with me."

Trapped? I held onto that bit of knowledge but made no comment on it.

"I saw you with the nymph," I said, calmly taking a bite from the tender meat of the bird. "If that is how you treat those you care for, I want no part of it." His growl covered most of his cursing. "She seemed to want no part of you, the second time. Her man stood woodenly nearby watching your use of her. Tell me, would you have raked her trunk like you do to the wood in here had she turned into a tree?" I motioned to the furrows dug deeply into the wood in the kitchen. The black cloud of mist containing him churned with his wrath.

Suddenly, the table and its bounty of food flew away from me as if pulled by a gigantic hand. Dishes clattered to the floor and shattered at my feet, splattering the gown with bits of food. Fork still in hand, I popped my last bite into my mouth.

He raged while I chewed, my heart hammering at my audacity. Still, I felt certain he wouldn't touch me in anger despite my words. He'd had opportunity to do so many times before. No, tonight was meant to tempt me to say yes to his offer. If he touched me, he knew the answer would never change.

"Thank you for the meal. I enjoyed the food, but the company could use some manners," I said lightly and stood, shaking what food I could from the dress.

I turned and carefully picked my way through the broken shards of dishware, navigating my bare feet to the safety of the bedroom. He growled, roared, and cursed the entire time.

Staying clothed, I lay back down in bed and stopped

listening to his rant. The meal and his tantrum had exhausted me. I went to sleep.

A<small>FTER PULLING</small> on my socks and then lacing up my boots, I crept to the kitchen. Disaster still claimed the room. On the butcher block, I spotted the shredded remains of my dress and bag. A small sack, about the size of my fist, waited next to the pile. I loosened the tie and looked in at the fine granules of real sugar. The dull, light tan crystals were a rare treat this far north and worth their weight in gold. Two gold coins rested flat against the table near the piled remains of my belongings. I imagined his temper after I slept and his regret after he vented it on my things. Shaking my head, I scooped up everything and headed toward the door.

I still felt weak, but no longer sick. Unsure of the quarantine, I hoped my arrival back in the Water would not cause issue. The vial of medicine, which had been on the chair when I woke, now hid within my bodice. I'd sipped a small dose when I had wakened, as a precaution.

Walking out into the sunlight, I filled my lungs with the fresh air and let it out slowly. A crow watched from a nearby tree, and I bowed to it. It clacked its beak at me in return. Smiling, I ambled to the gate, enjoying the feeling of the sun on my face. It didn't seem to happen too often inside the estate.

Ahead, near the gate, a figure hid under the shadows of the trees. I halted as soon as I spotted it, wondering if someone had crossed into the estate without the beast's knowledge. I didn't have many friends in Konrall, and those I had wouldn't risk the beast's punishment for trespass.

"Will you not consider my offer?" the beast called to me angrily. "I've sheltered you, fed you, cared for you. You have no cause to deny me."

Hearing his voice eased some of my fears, and I started forward.

"Stay where you are," he commanded angrily.

I stilled, wondering what madness gripped him now.

"Your answer. I will give you everything you desire if you but stay and do as I command."

"Everything I desire?" I fought to keep from laughing as he swore to it. "That is a foolish promise when you have no idea what I desire. What if my desire was your death or to destroy the manor? Neither would be possible, would they?"

He snarled at my logic, and I moved forward. He called me a spiteful woman, ungrateful and cold to the plight of others, selfish and cruel in the face of giving and kindness. As I neared the gate, he moved back behind the underbrush, trying to stay in the shadows. When I stepped onto the dirt just before the gate, he began to beg.

"Please," he said. "Anything that is within my power to give will be yours. Do not take another step. Turn back and stay with me."

I shook my head and stepped forward again. The gate swung open as he struck the tree under which he stood. With a roar, he trampled through the brush, and I saw the beast with no obscurity a moment before I passed through the gate.

His pointy ears shot up from each side of his head. His dark eyes were set deep under a dark, shaggy brow. Claws tipped each digit, and fur covered his entire body. With lips pulled back, his very sharp teeth gave no illusions as to what he was. He truly was a beast.

I ran. When I reached the road, I stopped and loosened my grip on the sugar and coins to switch to the other hand. My heart pounded in my ears.

In the distance, I could still hear him. They could probably even hear him in Konrall.

Knowing I'd made the right decision to leave when I had, despite my weak and shaking limbs, I set out toward the Water.

CHAPTER ELEVEN

A NAIL HELD A SIGN TO THE FRONT DOOR OF OUR home. Ignoring the quarantine warning, I let myself inside. A dry hacking cough greeted me, and I saw Father at the stove, cooking a watery soup.

"Benella," he cried, backing away a step. "You should have stayed away."

"No, Father. I couldn't ever do that." I moved toward him and plucked my vial from my bodice and set it on the table next to the other very low vial. "How much longer are you supposed to take the medicine?"

"Seven days from the onset," he managed before coughing again. The wheezing rasp at the end worried me. He looked drawn and pale. The hand that stirred the soup shook. I pulled out a chair, took the spoon from him, then guided him to sit.

"Where are Bryn and Blye?"

"Sick in their bed."

I found it odd that Bryn still lay abed when she'd been the first of us sick. I was already up and walking about the countryside. Keeping my thoughts to myself, I went to the well out back to fetch fresh water.

"The Head warned us not to go out during the day," Father said.

"We need water," I replied tartly. I didn't see how fetching the water only at night would benefit anyone. It just meant Father worked when he should be resting. If the Head cared so much, he could enter our den of sickness to scold me.

"Did you take your dose today?"

He shook his head, and I knew it was because there was so little left. How could the doctor think this would last seven days for three people when only a quarter of the vial remained? Father caught my expression as I carefully measured a dose into a cup and added water.

"Bryn took the dose twice a day hoping it would work faster. I suspect Blye did the same, but in hopes it would keep her from catching it."

I cast a glance at their closed door, the only consideration I gave them, and ladled some of the soup to Father. As he sipped it, there was a knock on the front door.

We both exchanged glances before I called out a quarantine warning.

"I know," a voice called back. "I put it there. So I'm wondering why we spotted someone entering this building a short while ago."

My eyes narrowed, and I jerked open the door. The Head stood in the road a good distance from the door.

"Good morning, Head. Please, won't you come in and discuss this transgression? Better yet, I will come to you, and you can properly reprimand me."

"Benella," Father scolded behind me in a whisper.

"Please stay where you are," the man said. "Now that you've entered, you may not leave until the sickness passes."

"I am fully aware of that. I can read," I said, pointing to the sign right beside me. "We are running low on medicine. The doctor said he had more if we had payment. We also need supplies: oats, flour, any greens to be found. Can you arrange for that? I'd rather care for my father than have to run any errands," I spoke softly, watching him to see if he understood my threat.

He nodded slowly.

"We can leave it on the porch and knock when you can come out for it. You have payment for it?"

Nodding, I turned away from the door and grabbed the two coins I'd set on the table. Father's eyes rounded, having just noticed them. At the door, I flipped them so they landed at the Head's feet.

"Boil them before you trade with them."

The Head reached into his pocket for a piece of leather and wrapped the coins within before walking away. He would probably boil the coins and burn the leather.

"Where did those come from?" Father asked when I closed the door.

I smiled and sat by him.

"You will never believe the story," I said, knowing full well he would.

Just then, the bedroom door opened, and Blye shuffled out. She coughed weakly into an embroidered linen square, no rasp evident in her exhale.

"I heard voices," she said pathetically to explain her presence. Then her eyes widened at the sight of me. "Benella, where did you get that dress?" She rushed forward and touched the sleeve of it. "Exquisite," she breathed and tugged me to my feet. "What happened to the hem?"

When she met my eyes, looking for answers, I asked a question of my own.

"Why are you still abed? You seem fit enough."

Her air of excitement immediately left her, and she again coughed into her linen square.

"I think I'm well and come from the room, but too soon I feel worn and shaky and need to rest. The illness teases me, giving me a moment of normalcy, then robbing me of it all within the same hour."

Probably just long enough for her to eat, I thought

nastily. I closed my eyes and pushed away my anger, knowing Father listened to us. It would do no good to pursue the subject.

"Then you should be back abed to rest. I will bring you something to eat soon. The Head went for supplies."

She nodded weakly and shuffled back into the room.

By DINNER, I'd made a hearty soup with the supplies delivered by the Head. He'd put the two gold coins to good use, and we had plenty to hold us for four days, including more medicine. I ladled Father and I each a healthy portion. He rose from his bed to join me at the table. I felt his forehead when I noticed an extra shine in his eyes. He felt too warm, and I recalled how I'd burned with a fever. After we ate, I helped him to bed, giving him a drink before directing him to call for me if he needed anything.

Then I took what remained of the soup, added cold water, and served the tepid watery mix to my sisters in bed. They took their bowls without comment and drained them while I watched.

The next day Father grew worse. I gave him another dose from my bottle, promising that any pain he felt in his lungs would soon disappear, and left him to sleep. For my sisters, I gave them their dose for breakfast and promised them food, soon. I delivered the food several hours later. More watered down soup.

An agonizing day passed, listening to Father's racking cough. I sat by his bed, just watching him breathe, and wondered if the beast had done the same while I suffered through my fever. By the time the sun rose, Father rested easier, and I made him drink more water before bathing his face.

At no time during the night had either of my sisters crept from their room, so I went to check on them as well. Both slept soundly, each on her own side of the bed, and I felt a twinge of guilt at my assumption that they faked a lingering illness. I waited until I closed the door softly before I let a small cough escape. Had Father not been ill, I would have been in bed last night as well.

Tiredly, I sat beside him again and soon began to doze.

As the days passed, so did the supplies. We all managed a full seven days of medicine, but remained in quarantine until Father's cough subsided nine days after I had returned home. By then, very little of the salted stag meat remained. When the Head declared us fit to open our doors again, we all worked together to clean and air out the cottage. I avoided the chore of boiling the linens and thought of the beast.

With supplies so low, my sisters whispered to me about going for more. They didn't ask how I came by the dress or why the Head gave us the food he had. They only knew that I'd been the source of the good fortune that helped us through the sickness. When their incessant pleading became too much, I snuck away at dawn to visit the sisters.

Father had returned to teaching the day before. Though I hadn't been to the Whispering Sisters in over a week, the guard nodded when he saw me and let me in. Ila greeted me just inside the door with tea.

"What brings you here today? I heard about your illness and am glad you're fit again."

I nodded in agreement and followed her down the stairs to the bathing room. After so long away, her nakedness drew my gaze again, but she didn't seem to notice. Aryana already lounged in one of the heated tubs.

"My sisters are making my ears bleed with their—" I took a deep breath and then lowered my voice to mimic their husky whispers.

"Could I bathe today?" I asked, instead of complaining.

"You are so self-contained," Aryana commented. "You need to let your thoughts out more often so they don't sour you from the inside."

She rose from the tub, and I held out a hand to help her.

"If I speak my mind, I will sour my family. I've grown used to biting my tongue over the years. It usually doesn't bother me."

Ila made a neutral noise as she led the way to the back

room. They shooed Gen out.

"Is this a new dress?" Aryana asked, touching the fabric.

I nodded and reached for the buttons running down the bodice.

"It's very pretty," she said. "I imagine Blye was quite jealous of it."

"How do you know Blye?" I asked, curious that she knew Blye well enough to know of her nature.

"Only what we hear from our clients," Ila whispered, helping me lift the dress over my head.

"Your clients speak of my sisters?" I didn't like that at all. Yes, I knew Blye could be a bit vain and jealous and Bryn a bit selfish and harsh, but they were my sisters. I loved them regardless.

"A few. They or their wives must see your sisters in the market district during the day," Aryana said on her way to fetch two pails of warm water while I discarded my underclothes.

Water cascaded over my head, and I raised my hands to wipe the water from my eyes. The touch of a hand on my back and another on my legs jarred me from my thoughts of a gossiping market street and to the reality of bathing with two relative strangers. My eyes widened a moment before Aryana slid her soaped hands to my shoulders. Her firm fingers melted my objection.

The past week of fetching, cooking, and cleaning had

caused knots and strains, which had helped inspire the visit to the sisters to soak in one of their tubs.

"You're still considered new in the village, so people will talk about you. They've commented on your good trading skills, too. Many wonder where you find out of season produce."

In that moment, I was very glad I'd hidden the sugar under my mattress at home. Perhaps I needed to alternate where I traded and ask the beast for more common items. What was I thinking? Was I going back?

A hand slid over my breast, distracting me. A tingle of awareness prickled my skin. It felt odd, but not painful, just wrong. I'd washed myself plenty of times and never gotten such a reaction before.

"Here," Ila handed me the soap, having reached my upper thighs. I was thankful she let me wash myself instead of continuing upward.

"You have more tension than most men," Aryana commented as she worked her way down my back. "Perhaps after a soak, you'd like us to soothe your muscles."

I recalled how Gen had reacted and politely declined. I caught Ila's knowing smirk, but ignored it. They rinsed me, and the three of us walked to the tubs, picking three close together. We didn't talk much. Too soon, Ila was insisting we get out before we made ourselves sick. We went to rinse with cool water, and they worked oil into my hair again after I dried by the fire.

WHEN I RETURNED HOME, the lingering smell of eggs and bacon tinted the air inside the cottage. Bryn stood before the wash pan, scrubbing the dishes.

"How did you get more food?" I asked excitedly, my stomach grumbling and eyes wandering, looking for what my nose smelled.

"I don't know what you mean," she said.

"Eggs. Bacon. I can smell it," the words took on a harsh tone as they tumbled from my mouth.

"Oh, yes. There wasn't enough to share. Sorry," she said airily as she set a pan aside.

"Did you at least give some to Father?"

"Please. He sits all day. I'm here cleaning, cooking, running to the market. I needed the food so I wouldn't collapse," she replied irritably.

She refused to turn and look at me. I frowned at her back. We had no food and no coin. Again. Trading away the sugar would be dangerous, but Father wasn't eating again. I went to the mattress and felt for the sugar, but pulled out an empty hand.

"Don't bother," Bryn said. "I found what you were trying to hoard selfishly and traded it for the food."

My mouth dropped open.

"A handful of sugar for only enough bacon and eggs to feed one?"

"Just go and get more," she said with a shrug as if I had come by the sugar easily.

I thought of the beast and his last, frightening appearance over a week ago. In all likelihood, I would not be welcomed back.

"I can't," I said desperately. "That was the last of it."

"Every time you leave, you come back with something new. Don't tell me that's the last of it. Go." She picked up a bag and threw it at me, her face twisted with anger and her eyes filled with tears.

I took the bag and left with nowhere to go. The sisters were now accepting customers, and I wouldn't enter the estate again.

Walking to the outskirts of town, I found a new patch of grass near a tree and sat there until the sun started to crest the horizon. Stomach cramping, I started the walk home.

Bryn looked up expectantly when I entered. I set my empty bag on my bed and went to the well to drink my fill of cool water. It stopped the hunger pains, for now.

When Father came home and saw no dinner waited, he grabbed a book from his shelf and left again. He returned a long while later with some grain. Bryn divided it and cooked half for our dinner.

IN THE MORNING, Bryn boiled the remaining grain for our breakfast and, looking truly concerned, insisted Father stay to eat his portion.

As we sat at our table, quietly appreciating the meager breakfast, a sharp rat-a-tat on the door interrupted the silence. Father rose to answer it while we all spun in our chairs to watch. No one stood at the door, but a piece of parchment lay on the porch just outside. Father retrieved it and brought it back to the table after looking up and down the street.

He scanned the note briefly, then gave us a small smile.

"There is a traveling merchant who just passed through the Water. He heard I might have some books I no longer need and offered a fair price if I bring them to Konrall today. He must continue through Konrall south before nightfall."

He quickly ate his last few bites and pushed away from the table.

"I will cancel my teaching for today and return shortly. The merchant also expressed an interest in meeting my daughters. You will accompany me." His tone allowed no argument, though I could see distaste in my sisters' eyes.

Thoughts whirled. My heart ached that Father had to give up even a single book to feed us. After being ill for so long and not working, there would be no pay for several days yet. Most scholars would count themselves lucky to still have a position to return to after an extended illness.

And a merchant wanting to meet us could only mean he'd heard of Father's desire to marry one of us off. One less mouth would relieve some of the burden.

Bryn tossed the dishes in the dry sink and hurried after Blye into their room. I ran my fingers through my hair before tugging it into a semblance of a braid, as usual. After Father returned, my sisters emerged from their room, looking fresh and well-groomed. Despite her illness, Bryn did not look as thin as the rest of us and still managed a healthy glow.

"Benella, can you carry these in your bag?" Father asked, plucking seven thin volumes from his shelves. Two were regarding the rudimentary teachings of mathematics, which I doubted Father even referenced anymore given his familiarity of the material due to repetitive teaching. Three regarded beginning reading and writing. The other two were rare pieces pertaining to flora and fauna. I didn't want to see them go.

"Did you procure a wagon?" Bryn asked, smoothing her dress.

Father gave her a flat look, and she dropped her gaze. The twit. We were selling his books because we had no coin. How exactly could he afford to pay for a wagon?

AHEAD, I spotted a familiar curve in the road clogged with

a thick, unnatural fog. We were close to the place where I'd cut through the woods to go to the estate when I'd still traded with the beast. How long had it been now? Almost two weeks?

"Father," I began anxiously. "Doesn't it seem a bit too warm for patches of fog?"

"It depends," he said absently, his breathing slightly labored. Typically a sedentary man, the long walk after just recovering from illness taxed him. "There may be cooler water hidden under the trees causing it."

The fog loomed closer, and I blinked at it, trying to determine if we were walking faster or if the fog crept toward us. Still several feet away, I caught a slight movement within the mist. Before I could call out a warning, hundreds of vines shot out, wrapping around us.

The thick fog consumed us, hiding us from one another. I heard my sisters cry out, and my father call our names. I was unable to answer as a vine wrapped itself firmly, but gently around my mouth, effectively gagging me. I bit down on the vine to chew through it, but the acrid sap that ran into my mouth worried me, so I spat out what I could and remained mute.

The vines tugged us through the trees, up into the canopy, ever closer to the estate while the mist continued to keep us isolated. I heard the growing concern in Father's voice when I did not answer his calls.

Fear bloomed in my chest. Could I still try to claim

refuge and would it work to protect all of us? How angry had my last departure made the beast? I felt the vines start to lower me and, soon, the mist retreated enough that we could see each other.

We all hung a few feet from the ground, tangled in vines. Bryn and Blye's eyes grew wide, and they began to struggle against their bindings when they saw we dangled inside the gate of the estate. Father calmly scanned the area, probably remembering his last harmless excursion behind the walls. The vines still binding my mouth worried me. I felt we would not leave this time without meeting the beast, and for a reason I couldn't guess, he didn't want me to speak.

The mist stopped retreating several yards away and then started to darken. Both my sisters began to cry. The pathetic mewling sounds had me pitying them and their fear. No one deserved to be tormented as the beast currently did to them. My eyes narrowed on the gloom, and I tried to speak around the vines, but it just sounded garbled.

"It would seem I have trespassers," the beast growled.

I snorted.

Father's face visibly paled, and he appeared to have lost his voice in the face of such menace.

"As the eldest, you shall take the punishment for the trespass, unless..."

I shook my head and attempted to speak past the gag,

trying to tell the beast to stop his madness.

"Unless, what?" my father said.

"Unless one of your daughters agrees to stay with me," the beast said.

I ceased my struggles, seeing what the beast meant to do, the sneaky son of a—

"No," Blye wailed.

"It's not yet your turn to answer," the beast snapped harshly. "The eldest speaks first. It's only right I offer her the opportunity. And, she should be grateful I consider her at all when she's carrying a bastard child."

Blye's sniffles stopped, and she turned to stare at Bryn. We all did. Tears trickled down Bryn's face, her shame evident. The food hoarding, the moods, and the request for a wagon made sense now. Pity welled up for her, and I glared at the beast.

"Come now. Your turn to answer. I offer you the refuge of the estate in return for your immediate and complete obedience in every command I issue. And your father's life, of course."

Bryn sobbed and shook her head. Had my mouth not been full of vine, it would have popped open. How could she not save Father? My eyes fell to her middle. Of course she couldn't, and Father would never have wanted her to, knowing she carried his grandchild.

"Very well," the beast growled with little menace. "Good sir, you should consider marrying her to the first offer you can manage before the soon-to-be husband discovers her state."

Father paled further and would not look at Bryn.

"Now, the next oldest," the beast said without compassion. "Your father stands to pay the price for trespassing for each of you. As you are aware, he will be thrown from the estate. Once for each of you. How do you suppose he will fair after the second toss? Or third? Do you honestly think there will be much left to throw the fourth time?"

Blye's mewling cry won her no pity.

"Please grant us mercy," she sobbed.

"I *am* by offering you this chance to save your father's life. Agree to stay with me. You will have the finest silks you can imagine in return for your immediate and complete obedience in every command I issue."

She wailed and begged for several long minutes before rejecting his offer. Through it all, Father said nothing, his eyes growing more despondent.

"Now," the beast said. "For the youngest."

The vines slipped from my mouth as he spoke, and I interrupted him before he could go any further.

"Release me so we may speak face to face. I will not speak my answer to your cursed mist."

Immediately the vines flew from me, and I fell to the ground. Straightening, I looked at my sisters and Father. They all had fear in their eyes.

"Benella," my father began. "Do not give up your life for—"

A vine slithered up from his chest to muffle his words.

Bracing myself for a confrontation, I walked straight into the mist and stopped when I felt a tug on my hair. My stomach gave an odd flip.

"What is your answer?" he rumbled softly as his fingers worked the braid free.

The heavy mist surrounding us muffled all sound, no doubt to keep my family from hearing. Though it also hid the beast from my view, I recalled every fang and claw in detail.

"Your terms are a bit steep for what you are gaining, and I would like to propose three revisions," I said bravely.

"How can they be steep?" he asked. "You gain your father's life."

"Do I? How do I know? That is my first provision. I must be allowed one day every week to leave the estate. If I'm not allowed to see Father, it will be just as if he had died."

The beast grunted in response. I felt him lean in to breathe the scented oil still clinging to my hair.

"What is your next provision?"

"I will ignore any command for my silence."

He didn't deny my provision.

"And the final?" he asked, instead.

"You may not touch me without permission."

His growl started low and grew in fury.

"Unacceptable," he roared. He fisted my hair and carefully pulled me against him so the fur from his jaw abraded my ear. "Why even keep you, then?"

I licked my lips.

"That's something I have been asking myself for many weeks. You've asked me so many times and offered so many things. Each time, I've said no. If you can't accept my terms, you will kill my father, I'm sure. Your temper will see to that. But you will lose any future chance of coercing an agreement from me. That I promise you."

He grew completely silent. I held still, waiting for his reply. Faintly, I heard Blye's continued sobs though Bryn tried to hush her, no doubt trying to hear what we said.

"A year," he growled. "I will accept your provisions for a year."

"No," I countered. "My silence cannot be guaranteed, and I will not lose my family. As long as I'm with you, you will listen to me and let me leave one day a week. In return for your gracious benevolence, I agree to reduce the touching restriction to six months." I had to raise my voice slightly so he could hear me over his own cursing.

Again, he stopped his rage. He didn't leave me waiting for long.

"One week."

I snorted.

"One month. That is my final offer."

"Agreed," he said, triumphantly.

"I would like to say good-bye before you start commanding me, sir," I spoke in a rush.

His fist released my hair.

"Make it quick."

Obediently, I rushed from the mist just as the vines released Father and my sisters. I went to Father first and hugged him tightly.

"I will see you in four days," I whispered to him.

"Don't do this, Benella," he said fiercely, hugging me.

"I'll be fine and well fed here." Pulling back, I caught the hurt look in his eyes and quickly tugged the bag from my shoulders. "Here. I'll try to find some way to help."

I turned toward my sisters.

"Take care of him." There was a threat in my tone that I hadn't meant to let slip. "And yourselves," I added more calmly.

Something tugged at my foot, and I lifted my skirt enough to see a vine.

"I have to go."

Turning, I walked into the mist, away from my family.

THANKS FOR READING DEPRAVITY, *Part 1 in the Beastly Tales. Benella's story continues in Deceit, Part 2. Keep reading for an excerpt from her life with the beast.*

AUTHOR'S NOTE

Thank you for reading Depravity! Beauty and the Beast is by far my favorite fairy tale. I've read so many different versions, the oldest ones having a merchant with six children (three boys and three girls). To me, the brothers didn't play much of a role in the story, so I stuck with the three sisters in this retelling.

As you read, the sisters are not created equally, and those personalities are going to continue to emerge and cause Benella grief. I can't wait for you to discover what's next for Benella and her family in Deceit, the second book in the *Beastly Tales*!

If you want to keep up to date on what I'm working on, sign up for my newsletter at mjhaag.melissahaag.-com/subscribe or join my facebook fan group, MJ's Curvy Cartel. Hope to see you there!

Happy reading!

Melissa

SNEAK PEEK OF DECEIT

Now Available!

Bryn's muffled sniffles faded as I stepped into the mists. I didn't go far before I hesitated. I could see the hand I held before me but nothing beyond that. Yet, visibility wasn't why I'd stopped. Fear held me in place.

The beast had always kept everyone at bay. Why had that changed? And, why with me? Knowing why he'd gone to such lengths to trap me within the estate might have assured me. Then again, perhaps his reasons were something to fear.

The beast's tail thumped against my stomach, a reminder of the bargain I'd made. To save my father, I had no choice but to clasp the tail and allow him to lead me through the mist. Walking away from my family was difficult, but walking toward my unknown future was harder.

Instead of leading me to the overgrown yard just outside of the kitchen, he turned slightly east. It wasn't long before gravel crunched under my feet. I frowned at the sound and at the sudden disappearance of his tail.

"Go where you wish within the boundaries of the estate. Do as you please, with the exception of leaving," he said, as he moved behind me.

The mist retreated with him and revealed a grand entrance to the manor that he so zealously protected. Three steps laid with large slabs of natural grey stone led up to a sheltered court. Great columns of the same stone supported a roof to protect guests who might arrive during inclement weather.

The claw-ravaged, large double doors stood open in invitation. Yet, instead of welcome, their gaping maw conveyed an eerie sense of desolation. With reluctance, I climbed the steps and entered the beast's home.

For the first time, I saw the interior of the manor clearly. Aged décor, perfectly preserved from the ravages of time, yet marred by the beast's anger and negligence, drew my curious gaze. Did he truly only need a maid?

"Should I clean, then?" I asked, knowing he still lingered behind me.

"Do as you please," he said irritably.

Taking him at his word, I went from room to room,

studying the place I would now call home. Though I did not care for cleaning, a good straightening would make it a fair place to live. As I wandered, I took time to right a tumbled chair or straighten thrown papers. In some places, shards of broken objects dusted the floor, and I made note to come back with a broom as my boots crunched over them.

I lost count of the turns and rooms I visited while the beast trailed me cloaked in his now small cloud of mist. Other than the library, I noted nothing of particular interest until I reached the second floor.

In the midst of the beast's destruction, a single room remained untouched, and I didn't blame him for avoiding it. Frills, perfumes, and pillows filled the room with their noxious pink shades. I had no issue with pink in small doses. However, what lay before me made my eyes hurt. The only exception to the overabundance, a set of black, glossy doors, called to me.

They were set into the interior wall to the side and begged for the beast's angry furrows. Yet, none decorated the surface.

I crossed the pink rugs and opened the door. On the other side, the wood bore the worst marks I'd witnessed, gouging so deep only a thin layer of wood prevented a hole. I gently ran my fingers over the marks, staring at the torn grains.

As I watched, a piece smaller than a hangnail twitched,

slowly straightening itself to mend the gash. I would have watched longer, fascinated by the display of enchantment, but the mess inside the room distracted me. Everything from the mattress and bed hangings to the inlaid wood patterns of the floor had been shredded.

"My room," he said from behind me. "This room is yours."

SERIES READING ORDER

Beastly Tales

Depravity

Deceit

Devastation

Tales of Cinder

Disowned (Prequel)

Defiant

Disdain

Damnation

Resurrection Chronicles

Demon Ember

Demon Flames

Demon Ash

Demon Escape

Demon Deception

Demon Night

More to come!

Connect with the author

Website: MJHaag.melissahaag.com/

Newsletter: MJHaag.melissahaag.com/subscribe

CPSIA information can be obtained
at www.ICGtesting.com
Printed in the USA
LVHW021542070922
727709LV00003B/439